M000304307

THE SON OF THE DEATHLESS
DEATHLESS
CHILDREN OF VASYLLIA

NICHOLAS KOTAR

WAYSTONE
PRESS

Copyright © 2022 by Nicholas Kotar

Interior book design by Heather Pollington

All rights reserved.

No part of this book may be reproduced in any form or by any electronic or mechanical means, including information storage and retrieval systems, without written permission from the author, except for the use of brief quotations in a book review.

❀ Created with Vellum

To Paul Kingsnorth.
May your roots grow deep.

CHAPTER

ONE

AN UNCANNY BIRTH

I n the land of Dunai, no one notices a golden sunrise any more than a fish notices water. But all Dunaians—human and non-human—come to attention at a purple sunrise.

The purple sunrise of Dunai comes on the same day every year. In a land with no clocks, time should be a flexible thing, dependent on the changing seasons. But what if there were a place where nature was in perfect harmony? Where the fallen impulses of human nature were tempered by a cycle of order, not chaos? In such a place, a sunrise can be a calendar.

But perhaps you are one of the unfortunates who has never seen a purple sunrise?

Imagine a clear morning in mid-March. There might be a bit of snow still on the ground, but the grass peeking through it is more green than brown. The mist rising from the ground leaves your fingers dripping with sticky wetness. Winter's usual lack of smells, on such a morning, gives way to the first scent of blossoms. A hint of lily of the valley, or maybe a whiff of eager lilac. Now look up at the horizon as the sun approaches.

Can you see that azure sky blushing pink at the approach of the sun?

Well, that pale line of pink is quaint compared to the fiery purple of the first morning of a Dunai spring. If there were a cosmic peacock that preened on the horizon, its tail feathers would fade to grey next to that purple. No shimmering aura of any borealis could hope to outshine it.

The purple morning of Dunai is a time fraught with the coming of new life into dead nature, but it is also a time of danger. The wise tell that the earth itself opens up like a gaping mouth along the riverbanks and swamp-fringes, feeding on care-less animals and people, gorging itself for the coming harvest.

And the mothers of children born on purple mornings gener-ally do only one thing.

They die in childbirth.

So when a purple morning marked the start of Pelaghia's labor-pains, you will forgive her if she was not entirely thrilled.

But Pelaghia had no intention of dying in childbirth. Not for what she was certain was a boy. Three girls she had given to Yan— a bristly, gentle giant who loved the person, not merely the vessel, of his wife. It was time for a boy, and everyone knew that boys born on purple mornings became the heroes of tales told for centuries. This son, predicted by Pitirim the village idiot (and secret wise man, as only a few knew), was the crown of their hopes. She ached to see those hopes in person, not merely to seed them with the power of her life's blood.

So she did what no birthing mother should ever do, especially on a purple morning.

She walked into the forest to give birth under the open sky.

Pelaghia was of an old Dunaian family that proudly traced its ancestry to an ancient time when Dunai had a different name. A name few remembered: Vasyllia, a land where gods and men used to live together in concord. A long, long time ago.

The ancient Vasylli had tales about children born on such days. The tale of the foolish Eremei who defeated an army while sitting on top of a stove. The tale of the cunning Mariska who outwitted the great Forest Mother using nothing more than a comb, a handkerchief, and an egg. The tale of Semyon the mad pillar-dweller whose dreams would accidentally move mountains while he slept.

All those tales had one element in common: the mothers of the heroes and heroines had been driven out of their homes, for various reasons, and were forced to give birth in the wild.

Pelaghia thought about manufacturing a proper scandal with Yan, so that he would throw her out of the house in a fit of pique. But Yan got red in the face—or at least the part of the face that wasn't covered by curls as black and glistening as bear-hide—from embarrassment, but rarely anger. No, it wouldn't work. She thought of perhaps starting a rumor with the old spinner-ladies in the common house. Something so shocking that the whole town would rise up and cast her out into the unknown. But even old women in Dunai were so placid that it would take a week's worth of simmering before anyone would so much as shout.

No, there was nothing else for her to do than cast herself out. So she did.

She took a thick wool shawl—the one with the pattern of acanthus leaves, not the loud pink one with the roses—and a basket with a few hardboiled eggs, a small wooden box of salt, a hunk of bread, and a block of cheese. She slung a blanket around her right shoulder and hung a few towels on her left arm. Then she waited for a moment when all three girls were busy about the house, and she slipped out like she used to when she was a miscreant of five.

Her getaway was stopped short by a contraction like a battering ram. She pushed the pain downward, breathed into her heels, and hummed the bass solo to a song that began with the words, "Was it my fault that my voice shook when I saw him?"

A song for lovelorn girls. *Not* one of the old ones. She felt silly and stopped singing.

The walk into the woods was uneventful. No man, woman, or

child so much as hooted at her. The earth did not open up to swallow her whole. She even breathed freely for a moment or so. Until she realized that would only provoke another contraction.

It seemed *everything* caused a contraction.

She walked for an hour, until the throbbing in her feet was unbearable. Then she sat at the edge of a shady clearing and ate an egg with some bread. In the middle of the third chew she saw something impossible. On the other side of the clearing, inside a sun-dappled stand of birches and alders, was a hazy pink light.

It was the most absurd thing she had ever seen. Naturally, she got up immediately to see what it was. Well, to say she got up is perhaps putting too light a touch on it. She heaved to her side, pushed up her bottom like a toddler sleeping on its stomach, huffed a few quick breaths, surged upward and immediately grabbed her belly (it had turned into a fire-heated torture device). When that beautiful dance had subsided, she waddled—even *she* would no longer call it walking—toward the stand of birches and alders.

A wind rumpled the crowns of the just-budding alders and the birch branches hoary with their spring earrings. The sun danced, and in that yellow-green light gnats hovered like dust motes. Under the gnats grew a circle of white flowers with petals edged blood-red. Each flower was a single stalk sprouting petals radially like a colorful hairbrush. Pelaghia knew the shape of those flowers. They were acanthus flowers, mirroring her shawl. Flowers there were in profusion, but no leaves at all, only stalks with petals, arranged in a nearly perfect circle that seemed to glow pink every time the morning rays shone through the trees enough to light up the white-and-red profusion, as though from within.

This was all very strange. Acanthus didn't grow in Dunai. Her shawl had been an exotic thing, a purchase from a Gruzina merchant at last year's harvest festival. But here was a fairy circle of acanthus flowers in a color she had never seen, in a place where no flowers should grow, at a time when nothing had bloomed yet.

Taken by a strange compulsion, she touched the petals. They felt spongy in her fingers, more like a fine mushroom than a flower petal.

The next contraction was so strong that she didn't have time to hum. She just screamed and entered the circle of flowers. Or, rather, it seemed that the circle itself moved, and she found herself in the middle, on her hands and knees. That helped a bit, and her scream subsided into a weary groan. "Pull yourself together, woman," she said. "It's too early to give up the birth-song! Or are you old already?"

She deepened her awareness, this time directly into her womb. She felt that oneness, that circle compelling itself into completion in her mind. And the song came to her without effort.

"Oh, in the fields of russet gold...the maidens came to gather flax..."

That was an old one. A good one.

The rest of what happened she barely remembered. Or rather, she had a sense, for years afterward, that the experience was so intensely real, so perfectly in the moment, that she had never really been alive before or after that morning. But the experience passed and left only a cloud in the memory. A pink-tinged, lilac-scented cloud, from which the cries of a healthy, pink-limbed boy resounded like the music of all the village choirs of Dunai combined.

Yan and the girls found her, leaning against an old willow tree, only an hour or so after the boy had been born. Already his eyes were open, and he was partaking of his mother's bounty with a gusto that made her laugh and her entire body glow as though it had an ember of coal burning inside.

In Yan's hairy bucket-hands, the boy was tiny. But in Yan's tear-streaked eyes, he was a giant.

"What shall we call him?" Yan asked, his voice breaking comically.

"Andry," she said, even before she had thought about it.

"Ah," he breathed out, contented. "A strong name. Good."

"He's going to need that strength," she said, her eyelids like lead weights.

She didn't see the way Yan's face clouded over at those words. She was already asleep.

CHAPTER

TWO

AN OLD SOUL

A ndry grew not in days, but in hours.

Well, that's how all the storytellers will speak of him in future years, no doubt. In fact, Andry did not grow faster than any of his sisters. He ate with more enthusiasm, of that Pelaghia had no doubt. But other than filling out his cheeks pleasantly and adding a few extra rolls between his hips and his knees, he was not an unusually large or strong child. Like all of his sisters, he had a period of about three months where he looked more like a frogling than a human, but then his lashes grew and his chin appeared. His eyes lit up with recognition at this new existence. Everything moved around him so unexpectedly, faces appeared out of nowhere to make strange noises at him. Best of all were the odd protuberances with spindly, articulated endings that twitched and danced before his eyes, without any apparent connection to himself.

Then, he seemed to recognize they were his own hands and feet, and something shifted in those bright blue eyes with a dusting of pollen-yellow around the iris.

He became beautiful, but not in the way of children. Most people, upon encountering a toddler (even an ugly one), will fly into paroxysms of silliness. Parents endure this, because they recognize the impulse to return to innocent bliss. But nearly every adult who approached Andry would begin that silly dance, only for their faces to change as soon as he looked at them. Their cooing and babbling deepened into silence and unblinking, long gazes into Andry's eyes. For a long time, almost an unbearable one, they would contemplate one another.

Andry would always be the first to break that long stare by smiling, and the effect was like waking up after a dream of flying. The stupefied adults all would reflect his smile, then walk on, as though drunk.

"He has an old soul, doesn't he?" they always said to Pelaghia. She smiled and nodded.

That pleasant strangeness surrounded Andry into his childhood. He played with other children as much as anyone, but there was sadness in his eyes sometimes when he was caught up in a game. As the other children burst into giggles, inventing their whimsical other-worlds, he would smile and play along. When they weren't looking, he would sigh wistfully.

Pelaghia saw it all and wondered. If he were to become a hero of a fairy tale, this tale would be an unusual one. So she started to collect her old books and stories to feed him on a diet of the wisdom of the ancients.

One early morning before the sun was up, she sat propped up against the log wall of the living room. As the dust from their chest of curios tried to slip into her nostrils, she saw Yan slinking outside.

Well, *he* would have thought it was slinking. But who ever saw a bear slinking?

He caught her gaze on the back of his head and stopped like a child caught in the act of spooning up the honey stores.

"It's nothing," he said, his face turning so red it was almost purple.

Then she saw that he was carrying three kettlebells in a single hand. She said nothing, only inclined her head significantly toward the guilty kettlebells.

He looked down and tried to appear surprised. Pelaghia couldn't help it. She exploded into laughter. He was such a child sometimes.

"He'll be a sensitive boy, my love," said Yan. "And even in Dunai, there are those who will laugh at him for it."

Ah, she thought. The man's solution to everything: bigger muscles.

But neither her solution nor Yan's seemed to do much good. Andry didn't grow to be wiser than his years. Every time his mother sat him down to read something from the old books, he would listen for a few minutes, entranced, but then strange things distracted him. An ant on the other side of the room, barely visible. A single bird call in the general cacophony of Dunai's songbird choirs. The scent of a rose petal wafting in on a breeze. Then he would lose all connection with her and the stories.

Nor did he grow to be bigger or stronger than anyone. Yan did his best, insisting—in his gentle, irresistible manner—that Andry play his "strength games." But though the boy was well put-together, he was small in stature and a little twisted in the back. So Yan had to stop pushing him, for fear he would do him lasting harm.

And it was as they both feared: the pleasant strangeness that had attracted others to him as a baby soon shifted into unease and, sometimes, open hostility.

ANDRY WAS close to his tenth birthday when the first subtle break in that year's winter came. He felt it as a familiar whisper behind the maple tree that grew next to the garden. Mother's vegetable beds were still covered by the layers of winter—snow, then leaves, then sticks, then manure that had long lost its pungency. This year, the whisper was more insistent than usual.

Strange. Usually, it was like a sleepy morning song sung by Kira, his middle sister. But today it was more like a sudden fall in a dream.

He investigated, thinking it might be a snowdrop. He should have known better, of course. Snowdrops don't whisper that loudly.

It was an impossible flower—radial white blossoms, edged with blood-red, sprouting from a tall stalk. And it was no longer whispering to him, it was singing. He touched it, entranced. It felt strangely like a thin mushroom.

Immediately, he was somewhere else. He saw Pitirim, the old man who hid his smarts under a blanket of craziness, digging like a dog looking for a bone it had hidden. His three and a half beard-hairs stuck out in all directions, and his bulbous nose, red as a radish, was dripping. A swipe across the nose, followed by an angry sniff, left a smudge of brown across his upper lip. It darkened his yellowish, stubbly mustache. His hands, already black with the never-washing, were crusted with icy dirt.

Andry *felt* the aching joints, as though he had put on a glove made of hardened bone that prevented his fingers from bending.

Pitirim stopped digging, listening intently. Then he turned to his right, and he looked right into Andry's eyes.

Andry leaned back in surprise, but realized he was somewhere else. He saw Elania, Goran the smith's daughter. She had green eyes that reflected the light of the fireplace. Her russet curls— Andry had a strange desire to touch them, to follow their waves as they edged her cheek—flowed unbrushed over her shoulders, which were bare save for a short-sleeved linen nightgown. She held a poker in her hand—that right thumb of hers was oddly wider than her left, something that Andry found inexplicably pleasant to look at—warming a piece of old bread with a slab of cheese and lard on it. The lard crinkled, wafting a sweet-salty smell. Behind her, Elania's mother Slaviana coughed wetly. She had been sick all winter with a wasting illness that made her look like a skeleton.

Andry *felt* Elania's stomach-pit, like looking over the edge of a hill that had no bottom. Fear and anger, but a strange, longing kind of ache, too. Then she looked out the window, and she looked... Pitirim looked...it seemed that the whole world looked... directly *at* Andry.

Andry blinked. He was in the middle of a forest he didn't recognize. At his feet was a fairy-circle of the same white flowers edged with red. But wait... those were not his feet, they were pointed in the wrong direction, pointed *at him*. They were huge, square-toed, leather. Boots of some kind. Uncomfortable, but dry. Necessary for the trek.

That last thought was so clearly not his own that he snapped awake. He was still standing in the garden, and now his feet were not merely cold. They were soaked through.

Still, he stood rooted in place, in spite of the cold damp in his feet. He had never before felt *people* like that. Flowers, sure. Rabbits and squirrels, naturally. Robins and kestrels and even eagles—he knew their alien minds and feelings as well as his own, and they loved him for it. But people? Never.

He had to figure this out. And he knew exactly who would help him.

PITIRIM WAS in the exact middle of town, still digging when Andry came up behind him. Two women with dirty skirt-hems were standing by the H-shaped wooden crank of the village well next to him, their faces pictures of disgust and amusement together.

The well stood slightly askew from the line of thatch-roofed houses framing this side of the village square. Directly across from Andry was the already-bustling market place with its rickety, spindly-legged stalls stacked next to each other like garden pots in winter. He was pleasantly surprised to see that a few of the early hothouse gourds were already being sniffed by the earliest grandmothers in their faded flower print pinafores. That might mean a stew of something delicious tonight.

Andry waited for the women to move away, chatting to each other conspiratorially as they looked back over their shoulders with sparkling eyes... this time at Andry. They were laughing at him for something. He never would have noticed that before. After all, who had time to notice such things when you could hear the moles talking to each other just under your feet? His head buzzed from the strangeness of *human* feelings, and he noticed that he didn't like that the women were laughing at him. He stopped, his mouth feeling fuzzy, his stomach queasy.

"A butterfly has sticks on its head, did you know that?" said Pitirim, still digging, his back to Andry.

That snapped Andry out of his stupor. He knew that the sillier Pitirim was, the more important was the message he was trying to give. Andry often wondered if Pitirim did it on purpose, or if he couldn't form thoughts and words in the same way as other people. More like a deer than a person.

He thought of an appropriate response. Sticks... butterflies...

"I saw a red salamander turn blue when I scared it," he said.

Pitirim stopped suddenly and turned his head to look at Andry. He looked like an owl that had suddenly woken up.

"That's right," he said, and breathed out in relief.

Then he plopped onto his buttocks and beckoned to Andry. Pitirim was wearing a long linen shirt, too thin for this early in spring, and too faded and dirty to tell the original color. His legs and feet were bare and his nails blackened with cold and dirt. His face was streaked with filth and the four tufts of hair on his spotted scalp seemed to be doing their best to avoid one another at all costs. But his eyes were clear and intent.

Andry sat on the icy dirt next to Pitirim. The old man scratched his nose in the oddest manner: he took it in his thumb and forefinger, as though checking to see if it was still there, then he twisted back and forth. It seemed to give him much satisfaction.

"Salmon returning to the spawning," he said, his voice rough. He looked sidelong at Andry, once again testing him. But Andry knew exactly what he was talking about now.

"Yes, my birthday is coming up. So what?"

Pitirim nodded sagely.

"Acanthia," said Pitirim. He didn't elaborate, but he did look away. Andry then saw that the strange flower was growing right at the side of the well. So it was real, then, not just a vision.

"Is that what that flower's called?"

"Bear-breeches," Pitirim confirmed with a silly smile. Andry had no idea what he meant.

"Not a flower," continued Pitirim. "When you understand that, then you'll have sticks on your head too."

He looked deeply at Andry, as though trying to think *at* him.

Andry breathed in and concentrated. Without prompting, the tip of his tongue came out and he bit it gently. It helped.

He heard the *kree-kree-kree* of a kestrel somewhere on the edge of town. Its dagger-wings cut the sky as it hovered in ecstasy. A kingfisher plopped into the river on the other side of the village, near the gorge where the old ladies claimed a mermaid lived. Two carpenter bees droned at each other angrily, fighting over the same scrap of wood outside the carpenter's shop. Stupidly, they avoided all the other scraps, of which there were hundreds.

And a thought plopped into Andry's mind.

It was that way with most people, wasn't it? They sensed each other much more than they sensed the world around them. Why hadn't he ever thought about that before?

Pitirim clicked his tongue. When Andry looked at him, he saw that the old man was very satisfied with himself. Andry smiled in spite of himself.

"The *best* salmon," Pitirim said conspiratorially, "always comes back to the spawning place on the *exact* day of its birth."

Andry screwed up his forehead in concentration. Did the acanthia have something to do with his birthday?

Pitirim hopped up on his feet, then grabbed his back in pain and hooted.

"Pitirim," said Andry. "Did you see the soldier with the square boots too?"

Pitirim stopped cold. He looked at Andry sidelong, nodded once.

"Harvest festival," he said. "That's the reaping."

Of course that's the reaping, but... Andry froze. The *reaping*.

What were the words that Otar Kalavan, the priest, sang at the Feast of the Farewell?

Those who reap men like wheat were abhorrent to Me...

Andry shuddered from cold and something else. He didn't understand. Not quite. And yet...

He turned to ask the question, but Pitirim was gone. Typical.

Andry looked at the acanthia plant, its petals almost aflame in the morning light. Something nagged at him. Something that he didn't realize but was very important.

Then... he knew.

When he had seen Pitirim in the vision, he had seen him exactly from the point of view of the flower.

Jumping up, he rushed toward Goran's smithy. As he approached, the smell of woodsmoke mingled pleasantly with the sweet smells of bread rolls from the bakery on the other side of the road. He stopped.

The acanthia was exactly where he thought it would be. He dropped down on all fours, so that his eyes were level with the petals. They smelled... fusty. Old, like... like mushrooms.

He looked up, and from the window of the smiths' house, Elania's laughing eyes caught his.

He ran away in terror. He had been *inside* the flower, seeing as it saw. But how could a flower see?

ANDRY RAN along the central road of the village, and the terror of the unknown groped at him. It was a like a scream inside his head, drowning out all the bird calls, the snuffles of rabbits in the hedges, the barks of elk in the tree-clad hills. His feet felt large and fuzzy, and his legs were heavy and stiff like wood. The people of the village looked at him with eyes that seemed to get darker the closer he came to them. Their heads twisted to follow him as their shoulders seemed to tighten with... what? Anger? Hatred?

He had no idea. It was all too terrifying.

He ran out into the snow-covered field set aside for that year's common wheat harvest. At the edge of it was his favorite archway of trees—yew and old oak and maple—through which he had long ago made a kind of path back to his house. It was safety, it was home.

But as he entered it, the trees loomed over him with claw-like branches. There were faces in the bark, leering with fangs that grew the longer he looked at them. Suddenly all of mother's stories, which usually he couldn't remember even when he tried, overwhelmed him like an entire week's worth of snowmelt falling on his head.

He screamed and ran on. Home. Home was just a few steps away.

But it was all wrong. The square log hut with its single gable carved with a cock's head no longer had windows with painted shutters. It had bulging yellow eyes that tried to suck his heart from his chest. He gasped, unable to scream any more.

The huge monster-head that used to be his house opened its vast maw, and there was a pit of horrible fire in its midst.

Andry's head spun and he fell.

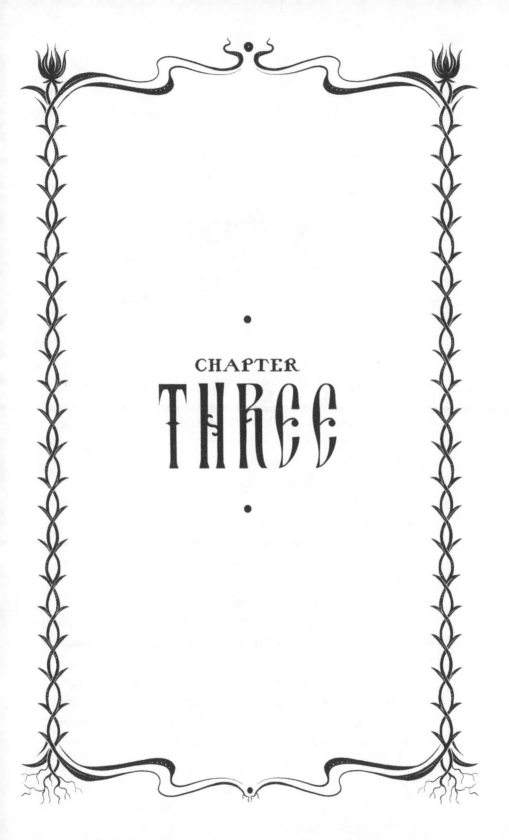

CHAPTER

THREE

THE LADY OF THE LAND

"I've told you, Mother. Again and again. But you won't do anything about it."

The voice was shrill and distant, like a mosquito flying around somewhere in a dark room.

"Hush, dear. You're not helping."

"I'm sorry, but maybe this was necessary. You and father need to see that Andry is not well. He's... strange... wrong in the head. You need to *do* something about it."

It was Aglusha, his third sister. She was fourteen and utterly convinced she was wiser than everyone else. Plumper than everyone else, too, with a sweet tooth to rival a butterfly's.

Mother let out a steady breath of air.

That brought Andry back. Mother was about to go into a dark mood if he didn't do something. The girls often had that effect on her.

But he couldn't open his eyes. The terrors in the trees, the glowering eyes of the villagers, the scream in his head—it washed over him again. But through it all, like a still, small voice in a crowd, he saw the acanthia. He held on to that image in his mind, and the fear cleared.

There were muffled sounds of shushing and the rustling of long skirts. Irena and Kira were comforting Aglusha now. So Mama must have said something.

"I might have expected my own *daughters* to form ranks to protect their baby brother!" That was definitely Mama. She was not happy.

Andry clung to the image of the flower. It was like someone unclenching a hand inside his chest. He breathed and it came out like hissing.

The sounds all died down.

"He's alive," whispered Mama. He could hear the tears in her eyes.

"Out!" said Papa in an exaggerated stage whisper.

The fluttering of skirts increased, then the door creaked and slammed shut.

Andry tried to speak, but no words formed on his lips. They stayed in his head, as though there were a physical obstruction between his thoughts and his mouth.

And least he could still form thoughts in his head.

"You don't think..." began Papa.

"Yes, I do," said Mama. They often talked in half-sentences like this. It drove the girls mad, but always made Andry feel warm and protected.

"Should I...?" That was Papa again.

"No, it must be my burden."

That scared him. When Mama talked like that, it meant she was thinking of the old Vasylli ways. The ways that had long ago died, along with Vasyllia.

But the flower in his mind was now a fairy circle glowing pink in a dappled glade filled with birches and alders, leaves shuddering in a breeze.

He felt a new thing. It was heavy, like being sad. But it was also exciting and a little scary. He tasted honey cakes with lavender frosting and heard the church bell tolling on harvest night. It was sad and happy at the same time. He felt the tears form on his eyelashes, but he wanted to laugh too.

"Look," whispered Papa. "I think he can hear us."

"Hurry," Mama said.

MAMA'S HEART beat so hard, Andry could feel it through her breasts. She was half-humming, half-singing in that way she did when she wasn't thinking of the music, but was focused on something else. It was all wrong at first, frenetic and hissing. But as he allowed himself to melt into her breasts and soft belly, her voice firmed. He could hear words now, not just the hissing. A song he didn't know, though it felt old, like that ache in Pitirim's bony hands. It was like drinking slightly soured cider on a fall evening at the common bonfire. A safe feeling. Andry decided to try opening his eyes.

His body didn't listen at first. He knew why: he was afraid he had lost his eyes as well as his tongue. But the light behind his eyelids had been getting redder and brighter, so he willed his crusted eyelashes to break open.

He saw... Mama's nostrils, flared. Her second chin, shuddering with her rushed walk. A single hair riding the tip of her nose. He could tell by the pink in her cheeks that it was tickling her like crazy. Without thinking, he reached for it, to move it aside. The whites in her eyes brightened and her eyes got moist, suddenly.

Only then did he realize that he could move again.

The rattle in her chest as she coughed between hums and snatches of song gave her away. She was about to cry again. He tried to smile and looked away.

The forest was rolling up and down pleasantly around him. Most of the trees had budded already, and the smaller trees and bushes were sporting that bright gold-green that hurt him if he looked too long at it. There were even occasional snatches of red and blue here and there as the inhabitants of the understory came to lazy life again.

Andry realized only then that Mama had been carrying him for a long time. She was a strong woman, stronger than her pudgy arms and persistent baby-fat suggested. But she wasn't strong enough to carry him this long, was she?

He tried to adjust his body in a way that would let her know he could walk on his own. But his legs were still like cold jelly. Her arms just pressed him into her chest more firmly.

He sighed and closed his eyes again. He was so tired.

Then her hands twitched around him, ever so slightly. He came suddenly awake as the sweat sprouted on his forehead and his heart hammered.

He opened one eye.

The salmon has returned to the spawning place.

There it was, just as Mother had described it: the fairy circle of acanthia flowers on their tall stalks, not a leaf in sight. They glowed pink in the dusky sunlight.

"Impossible," she whispered. She wasn't speaking to him, he knew.

She was trembling now. A single drop of sweat rolled off the tip of her nose and fell onto his hands, hot to the touch. That same strange, heavy feeling of sweet sadness washed over him again. He sobbed, unable to stop himself. He didn't want to stop himself. It felt good.

"Here goes," she said.

She put him into the circle like he was a toddler, onto his back.

The entire forest for miles around, with all the villages of the Dunai, all their animals, people, plants, insects, underground creatures, even the water and air—they were all inside Andry at once, and he was inside them. They were the same, single being. But no, that was wrong. They were all part of a larger thing, something big, warm, like a huge blanket or like the biggest, softest feathered wing he had ever touched.

Andry closed his eyes.

He had always known that Dunai was special. Deer grazed together with domesticated goats in the pastures. Toddlers played with wild rabbits and squirrels under the eaves of their houses. Wolves were known to come to the edges of the storyteller's fire pit and sit together with the dogs. On sunny days, as the spinner-women worked outside, songbirds landed on their shoulders and sang to them in rhythm with the humming wheels.

And now he knew why.

It was not a reason. It was a person. He was looking right at her.

She swayed like the trees, or rather *with* the trees. Her skin was nut-brown. In the places where the dappled sun lit her skin, it resembled treebark, but in the shadows, it darkened to the hue of freshly-turned compost. Her ridged skin was laced in places with pink and orange lichen that looked almost like fabric. Her hair was golden and green and brown and... he couldn't find the right words. His mind offered comparisons—mushroom caps, moss, ivy in high autumn, honeysuckle—but it was none of these and all of these at the same time. She smelled like the autumn feasts of Dunai—sweet as honey and rich as mushroom broth. All around her, music hovered like motes of pollen or cherry blossoms falling.

She smiled. Andry recognized that smile. She *was* Dunai. Andry remembered once seeing a tree broken by an ice-storm in winter. The following spring, when he saw it again, trailing vines had grown from the ground, hugging the ailing trunk, slowly. Other trees nearby leaned down to it. By the season after that, the broken tree trunk had been buffered inside a nest of vines, propped up by the branches of other trees like a splint holding a broken bone together. Soon the tree that had cracked in half was once again a living thing.

She had been the voice that had sung that song of healing.

Now, she held a bouquet in her hands, extending it to Andry. It was acanthia in profusion he had never seen. Its soft mushroomy smell mingled with her own aroma of lilac and upturned earth. He reached out to her, oblivious of anything but her presence.

"Fascinating," said a foreign presence with a voice like a wind in alder-leaves.

Andry realized his eyes had been closed this entire time. He opened them.

There they were. The square-toed boots from his vision. For a moment, his head spun. Where was he again? Was he looking through his own eyes or the eyes of the blossoms? Where was the lady of the land?

It was a little too much, and he felt himself go fuzzy again.

The last thing he heard was the gasp of his mother.

"*KREEK!*"

The sound was a stab of excitement in Andry's gut, a familiar presence. It was the voice of a kestrel, his favorite bird of prey.

Then it all came back to him in a rush, and he jumped up.

His sister Aglusha yelped.

"Well, that's quite a young man you have there," said a voice with a hidden chuckle in it. It was the same voice that had whispered like alder-leaves. The voice belonging to the square-toed boots.

Andry was back at home, lying huddled on the stove-bench like a little baby. Mama, Papa, the four girls, and two unknown men sat at the table in the main room. Papa was tense, Mama looked ready to collapse either into giggles or weeping, depending on the next few moments. Everyone... *Everyone* was looking at him.

"Hello," said Andry, feeling his face get hot, imagining it beet-red like Papa's.

Something snapped in the air like a bowstring pulled too far. Everyone laughed.

It was the wrong response. Everything about the room was wrong: the way Irena leaned on her elbow, the way the plates, heaped with steaming crepes, were arranged on the table, the wide eyes of Kira as she laughed more loudly than the others, on purpose.

The wrongness lingered, giving Andry a chance to look at the strangers. Square-toed boots was an old man with a short white beard and sad eyes. His head was elaborately wrapped in some kind of silver-fringed black headdress. It was like a frame for his green eyes, filled with strange depths that shimmered with shifting emotions. Sadness but anger but also laughter. He was dressed in a woolen black kaftan with silver embroidery across the chest. It seemed to be more than decoration—something with meaning, like a script in a language Andry didn't recognize.

Magic? Yes, that must be it. That old man was a magician.

And to top it all off, the kestrel that had woken up Andry sat on the table next to the old man, as though they were not just friends, but connected somehow, staring at Andry. Its eyes were the same as the old man's. That made Andry jump.

The kestrel and the old man both leaned back at that, as though recognizing something they shared with Andry.

He had to look away. There was danger in their eyes.

The other man, though. He was worse. A young man with mustaches larger than his lip, twirling like ivy fronds. They didn't move with the rest of his face. Neither did his eyes. They were dead, like bits of amber stuck in a living face. Andry's gut coiled at the sight of him. He was looking not at Andry, but at the old man, with the intensity of a snake about to pounce on a mouse.

Andry's family continued to laugh.

"Come, join us," said the old man. He said it like it was *his* house, his table, and Andry was his guest. Andry's gut twisted again. But he complied, coming down from his bed and walking with shaking legs toward the common table. The smells of fresh dough and boiled eggs beckoned, though he expected even those familiar scents to be lying to him somehow.

Then he realized what was happening and felt his eyes go wide, even as he tried to stop them. Both the men, the old and the young, had greaves of polished steel and gauntlets hanging off their forearms, attached by cords of leather. Chain mail chinked under their clothing as they moved. Of course. These were soldiers of Karila.

That would explain why Papa was so tense. Papa had always made sure to tell Andry that Dunaians didn't hate Karilans. But he'd said it in such a way that Andry thought maybe Papa was lying, or at least covering something up. Andry tried to remember what Mama had told him about the lands around Dunai. He was bad at the details, and looking at the young soldier with the eyes like cold amber, he realized now that is was dangerous not to pay attention. What had Mama told him?

She had said that Karila was a great power, though Andry didn't quite understand what she meant by that. Was it because it was a big country with a lot of power, or did it have the best armies? Or was its power magical?

One thing he did remember. It was that Karila called itself a Protectorate. But whenever Mama said that word, Andry had felt that she wanted to spit. So it was one of those words that mean the opposite of what it seems to say. One thing Andry knew: if someone like that young solider came to your town to offer protection, you might be better off running into the woods.

He tried to listen to the conversation going around the table. His mind was still a bit fuzzy, and he found himself oddly focusing on single words or phrases and losing the thread of the larger conversation.

Then he heard his father say the phrase, "forever-war." It made the young soldier's face flush with anger. Something in Andry's mind clicked. He remembered one of Mama's lessons.

The forever-war was the terrible thing that no one talked about, but everyone knew. Nebesta, the country closest to Dunai to the south, had been one of the lands that decided it didn't want Karila's protection any more. But Karila didn't agree, and tried to force Nebesta to be protected. At first, it worked. But the Nebesti, in Mama's stories at least, were like little boys who refuse to be told what to do and only wait for you to turn around before doing the exact thing you told them not to. So they went into the hills and hid. But they kept on fighting from there. Little battles, here and there. Mama had explained that that sort of war was the worst, because those who suffered most were the common people in the cities and villages of both lands.

But Andry knew that Dunai was largely left alone by both. He wondered why. Did it have something to do with the lady of the land? Did she protect them?

The conversation going on around Andry at the table grew more animated. The young soldier was trying to convince Papa of something, waving his hands comically (his eyes still didn't match either his tone or his spinning arms). Papa was having none of it. His face was pink, and Mama was starting to drum her fingernails on the table in annoyance. She was trying, Andry knew, very hard *not* to look at Andry. Not to betray that she was worried sick about him and Papa and everyone.

"We've not had a single Nebesti incursion in Karila proper for over ten years!" insisted the young soldier.

"That's not what I've heard," said Papa into his beard.

The young soldier guffawed, offended. "You Dunaians. So above it all. So high and mighty. I mean, what other people would dare, in all seriousness, to insist that they don't need to hunt? Isn't that right? You peace-loving fools. You probably eat nothing but plants."

"Oh no!" burbled Aglusha, her eyes like still pools reflecting nothing but that soldier's handsome face, "I've seen it myself! Anything from a grouse to full-antlered elk with shoulders as high as a man's head—they come to the edges of the villages to die. They simply lie down and breathe their last. Those offerings of the land are then distributed to everyone in the village."

"*Offerings of the land?* How quaint," sneered the solider, looking not at Aglusha, but at Irena, the eldest. For a moment, there was something like a spark in those still-dead eyes. "The paradise of Yedem come to the realm of Earth, right? I bet your gardens weed themselves!"

"It's true!" Aglusha leaned forward, oblivious that the soldier was mocking her. "Well, not quite. We do have weeds, but they're easy to pull out. They almost jump into your hands! And you know what they do when you put them into a pile?"

Unwillingly moving his face away from looking at Irena— Andry noticed his oldest sister's pale-blond eyebrows were *very* arched and each of her cheeks had a perfectly round circle of flush—the soldier looked at Aglusha. He might have been looking at a spider he was about to step on.

"No, *do* tell," he said, adopting her lilting tone, to Kira's malicious amusement. Andry's middle sister—her black eyebrows like caterpillars climbing across her forehead— also had eyes for nothing but the young soldier. Now that he noticed it, he saw that everything about the girls—their move- ments, their glances, the emotions that Andry could now sense like waves of scent—were focused completely on the young man. It was sharp and unpleasant, like opening a bottle of soured milk.

"Well," Aglusha settled into her storytelling mode—hands splayed out and mouth comically open—"in other places, people burn weeds and dead branches of trees, yes? Not here! Here, you just pile them up off to the side of the fields. In a few months, they're not ugly piles of dead plants any more. They turn into compost!"

The young man's attention deepened subtly at that. The pres- ence of the old man seemed to grow in Andry's peripheral vision. They were both listening intently to Aglusha. Naturally, she was loving every minute of it.

"So the abundant harvests," said the young solider, "the size of your vegetables, the fabled Dunai horns of plenty... they're not just exaggerations, are they?"

Andry had an intuition that the young soldier was speaking to the old man, though he was looking at Aglusha, who now began to wither a little under his almost lidless gaze.

"Only fools disbelieve old tales," said the old soldier, simply.

The young man's cheeks colored with a wash of pink, then faded again.

"Which tales?" asked Mama. She was looking at the old man with unusual intensity.

The old man leaned down to look at the kestrel. The bird cocked its head, as though thinking. It raised one foot and *kreeked* loudly. The old man nodded as he slitted his eyes in thought.

"Matron," said the old man. "Did you know that those flowers —the acanthus-like white blossoms with the blood-edge—grow nowhere else in the land of Dunai?"

Mother shook her head once, tentative.

"In fact," the young soldier interrupted. "They grow nowhere else in the world, as far we can tell."

Father shifted in his chair. It creaked under him as though it were about to break from *his* strain.

"Why is that important?" asked Andry, before he realized that he had said it aloud.

"This land is very special, young man," said the old man. His eyes said something else, though. They said, "It means that *you* are very special, young man."

Andry's heart felt like it was doused in icy water. This old man was the really dangerous one, he was sure of it.

The old man looked at him for a long second before turning to Papa.

"Sirrah, I have a desire to see the village. Would you give me your son as a guide?"

"Andry? He's a boy. I will gladly show you around." Papa was pretending to be calm. But the line of sweat under his brow was betraying him.

"I think not," said the old man. "Something tells me this young man would give me a much better sense of the place."

Andry did not like that phrasing one bit. The old man knew too much. Clearly a wizard. A bad one.

To Andry's shock, Father nodded.

"We are at your service, sir," he said, bowing his head.

That was the scariest thing Andry had seen yet.

CHAPTER

FOUR

THE KILL

Andry and the old soldier walked through the village side by side. He had never thought of it as anything other than home. But now, the wrongness filled him again. The squat log buildings covered in old thatch had always felt like kindly grandmas waiting to embrace him. Now they looked like diseased crones, their gaping mouths missing teeth. The dusty roads were no longer straight, but just a tiny bit curved in a way that made Andry sick to his stomach.

The people stared at both of them with eyes that seemed all whites. Had they always had such long faces and cavernous cheeks?

Even the common house for the widows and old cripples, in front of which the fires for storytelling night often burned with an applewood scent, now slapped him with a stench of vomit and excrement. Disgusting.

It was all too much. This wasn't normal, this wasn't what Andry's experience of every day was like. What was happening to him? Was the old man playing tricks with his mind? Some kind of dark magic?

But the old man, as though released from some bond now

that he was alone with Andry, looked serene and still, his arm cocked up for the kestrel to sit on comfortably.

Had Andry been wrong about him? He didn't feel so dangerous now that he was apart from the young soldier.

The kestrel on his arm cocked its head back and forth comically, its eyes huge. It was like it was trying to absorb everything at once. *That* Andry understood. At least he had one kindred spirit in the odd group of visitors.

The old man interrupted Andry's thoughts.

"Do you like to swim, young man?"

Andry certainly did, and he felt himself glowing on the inside at the thought.

"It's a bit early in the season, but I can show you some of the best spots."

"Lakes or rivers?"

The sudden intensity of the old man's face didn't fit the lightness of the question.

Andry froze for a second. He felt like he was being quizzed on something that he should know. It would be extremely embarrassing if he got the answer wrong.

"There's one lake by the foot of the mountains. It overflows into a lot of little rivers during the spring, especially when it rains. But in summer there are usually three main rivers flowing from it."

"Flowing *from* the lake? Really?"

Andry nodded, but he was sure he got it wrong, that the old man was about to laugh at him.

"So what feeds the lake then? Rainwater? Or underwater springs?"

Andry breathed out loudly. He hadn't realized he had been holding his breath. Chuckling at himself, he felt his body relax. He knew the answer to this one.

"It's fed by the mountain. Here, I'll show you... sir?"

Andry felt foolish again. He didn't know the proper address for a soldier of Karila. Why, oh why didn't he pay attention to Mama's lessons?

The soldier's mouth quirked on one side only, but his eyes softened for a brief moment.

"The way a Dunaian should address a nobleman of Karila is 'my lord'."

Andry felt his eyes grow wide and his stomach shrivel.

"But you can call me Apsat. My rank is Vohin."

So, an officer, then, not a magician. At least not an officially trained war mage.

"Pleased to meet you, Vohin Apsat," said Andry, extending his hand in the Dunaian greeting. The old man looked at his hand in confusion for a moment, then seemed to remember. He took Andry's arm above the wrist and gripped firmly. Andry smiled and gripped back.

The old man was smiling fully now. Andry couldn't help it, he was starting to like the dangerous old magician. He still thought of him that way, couldn't help it.

The way to the best overlook in the area was not by any of drovers' paths trampled to dirt by the sheep and cows. The best road was an old hunting track, from an age when Dunaians still hunted. No one remembered it existed except Yan and Andry. Every month of the growing season, Yan would take an old war-adze and Andry a long knife, and they would take an afternoon to keep the way clear of branches and thorns.

There was little grass in this part of the forest, which was mostly old oak and maple with blackberry growing in clumps here and there. In the winter, the path was light-filled and so open that Andry always felt like he could reach up and actually touch the clouds. In high summer it was green-dark and whispering, a place that kept its secrets to itself.

Now, in the early spring, it looked like there were little flames of green on brown torches everywhere.

He led Apsat up the path as it twisted with the curve of the land, following a natural incline toward the first of two peaks that sat like a saddle above the village.

"There!" said Andry, puffing only slightly. The old man's

breathing hadn't changed at all, as though he had floated, not walked, up the hillside.

Below them, framed like a picture by two massive moss-streaked elm trunks, was the lake. It was long and narrow, curved like a new moon, with a single tree-clad island in the center of its right curve. It was now fed by what looked like hundreds of rivulets coming down the mountain, polished silver like Apsat's plate-mail greaves in the still-brown of the land. Beyond the lake, the upland plain rushed toward the distant peaks that were the northern edge of the Dunai.

The old man was trying to contain his excitement, but his twitching eyelids and clenched fist gave him away. His dangerousness flared again in the intensity of the kestrel's gaze.

They weren't looking at the lake at all. Nor were they looking at the border peaks. They were looking above them.

Andry tried to look as well. But he couldn't. His eyes simply wouldn't lift higher than the peaks. They stopped, and his head would not move higher, nor would his eyes tilt upward.

That was very strange.

He screwed his face up and forced his eyes up. He yanked his chin up with the flat of his hand.

At first, it was all blurry and sun-streaked, like water when the sun is reflected in it. His insides were screaming, "Don't look! Don't look!"

He closed his eyes again, breathed deeply, and saw the face of Dunai, the lady of the land. She looked tense now. He asked her, inside his head, to let him see it. Whatever it was. She sighed, but nodded.

He opened his eyes and saw something he had never seen before. Even though he had been in that spot countless times.

Beyond and above the border peaks, which were still clad in winter, there was a wall of stone that seemed to have no end as it reached into the clouds. It was yet another mountain range, higher than any mountains had any right to be. Those mountains were so sheer that they had no snow on them. But they were streaked with silver all the same. Water. Water falling down the walls of stone like flowing tears. Here and there some of the larger falls seemed to be giving off steam.

"Could it be?" whispered Apsat to himself. He looked at the kestrel, which had hunched its shoulders, ready to fly. It opened its beak and unfurled its wings slightly. They looked like two drawn swords at its side. As small as a turtledove it was, but Apsat remembered that, outside of Dunai, it was a killing machine all the same.

Apsat seemed to come to some sort of decision, but his eyes were heavy and his breathing hard. He looked like he was in pain.

"Vohin Apsat? Are you alright?"

Apsat didn't react. He sighed deeply, then nodded and clicked his tongue. The kestrel shot off his arm and into the trees. It screamed, and something thumped hard behind Andry before he had time to turn around.

It sounded like Aglusha punching the pillows when she was mad.

Andry's heart was pierced with icy pain. He clutched at his chest. It was difficult to breathe. Apsat took him by the shoulder roughly and pulled him down toward the trees.

"I'm sorry, boy," hissed Apsat. He was more dangerous now than ever, his eyes hungry for something that Andry had no words for.

The kestrel was *kreeking* on a pillow of yellowing leaves under an alder tree. But no, they weren't leaves. They were grey-yellow feathers. Andry's heart squeezed in pain. The kestrel had killed a tiny goldfinch.

The wrongness inside Andry was like the land itself screaming in pain. He closed his eyes and saw Dunai. Her hands were bloody, and she wept brown-flecked tears. Andry's eyes filled with hot tears, and his chest heaved. He loved those small birds. They were like oversized bumblebees.

At that moment, he hated Apsat.

"Forgive me," said Apsat.

He wasn't looking at Andry, though. He was speaking to Dunai.

"Can you see her too?" Andry asked in a whisper that was interrupted by his own loud sob.

The old man, who had been avoiding his gaze, finally looked at him. His eyes were red-rimmed and wet.

"No, I cannot. I do feel her in the pain of the land. But it is necessary. Look."

The last word snapped like a command, and Andry felt his head jerk downward.

He gasped aloud. A fairy circle of acanthia flowers had appeared around the kestrel and the dead finch. The stalks were no longer leafless. Or rather, they didn't have leaves, but fronds with tips that looked sharp like needles.

"Come," Apsat half-sang to the kestrel. There was urgency in his voice now, and a little bit of fear.

The kestrel cocked its head at him and didn't move.

The fronds ... moved. They danced and grew longer, right in front of Andry's eyes. They were growing *toward* the kestrel, points-first.

"My heart," whispered Apsat, his eyes shut in concentration. "Come." The "m" of the last syllable he hummed, and it turned into music.

The kestrel, its beak open and its tongue darting out almost like a dog panting, flew up and hovered over the finch, twittering and shuddering in mid-air. The fronds retreated. It was strangely hypnotic, but beautiful. New music rose between the gusts of wind, something like a reed instrument or a whistle. It didn't feel natural. It felt like someone huge and invisible was tuning a flute.

As the kestrel returned to Apsat's arm, something gurgled from the direction of the fallen finch. Andry didn't understand at first what he was seeing. There was a seething mound of what looked like insects that had come from nowhere and covered the finch. Then the ground itself seemed to open like a mouth and the finch, still seething with the insects, fell into the ground as its lips closed again over the place where it had been. The acanthia flowers... bowed toward the center of the circle. Andry was moving toward the center even before he realized what he was doing.

Apsat held him back. "Wait," he said.

Nothing changed for a second. A minute. Ten minutes.

Apsat was frustrated. He shook his head once, as though he were having an argument with himself. Andry knew how that felt.

Then he extended his hand toward the fairy circle, palm-up. He whistled, and it harmonized with the flute-music filling the gaps in the noises of the forest. The music swelled, and now Apsat seemed to be conducting it with the fingers of his outstretched hand.

The earth... shuddered.

The acanthia petals lost their color and shriveled right in front of them. The earth pulled itself into a lump like a bunched tablecloth, and the mouth opened again. The finch flew out, singing in unison with the music of Apsat's whistling.

"I knew it," said Apsat, and his voice was joyful but tense at the same time.

The finch had come back from the dead. Dunai had given it new life. Andry's mouth was hanging open, he realized. He shut it, embarrassed and sneaked a look at the old magician.

But Apsat wasn't looking at him. His eyes had a vague look to them, as though he were listening more than looking. Andry closed his eyes and listened too.

There is was. Growling. Roaring. And it was coming closer fast.

"Well, then! Quite a personality you have, my lady." He laughed dourly. "Come, boy. Unless you want to be eaten by something with very long teeth."

He turned and ran back the way they had come.

CHAPTER
FIVE

THE LIVING LAND

A ndry was buzzing with questions, but Apsat ran as
though he were being hunted. Which, judging by the
roars growing louder behind them, was exactly what was
happening.

Andry couldn't help himself. He was thrilled. Something very
important had happened. Now if only the old man would stop
long enough to explain what it was.

"Why did you make Dunai angry?" Andry finally asked, raising
his voice to make sure the old man heard him.

Apsat stopped in his tracks and looked back at Andry with
raised eyebrows. Was it the question he hadn't expected? Or that
little ten-year old Andry would ask it? The adults never expected
him to understand anything. As though all children, especially
him, were stupid by nature until they magically became wise
with age.

"I provoked her, yes. And if you would tell her I'm sorry, I'd be
grateful. But I had to make sure."

Then he turned and ran back down the hill, avoiding the trails
entirely, just bursting through bushes and shrubs in a straight line
down the hill.

Andry ran to keep pace, grateful that the old man was clearing a path for him. Still, he nearly fell several times. It only added to the exhilaration. His smile started to hurt his face, it was so wide.

Since the old man wouldn't oblige, Andry forced himself to think as he ran. There were stories told by the storyteller's firepit that suggested the reason there was hardly any sickness in Dunai among humans or animals was that the land consumed the sick. Swallowed them up. Even, some of the more mischievous old crones suggested, bad little children were swallowed up sometimes. But they always chuckled at the horror in the kids' faces, so he thought they were probably exaggerating.

But this was different. What if the land didn't consume, but cured the sick and weak? But was it Dunai that raised the bird from the dead? Or did Apsat?

And another, niggling thought at the back of his mind that seemed not important at all, except it probably was more important than anything else.

Why had the old man been so interested in the source of the lake-water?

Apsat stopped, barely winded from the run, at the foot of the hill on the outskirts of the wheat fields. He plopped to the ground at the foot of an old yew, and leaned back contentedly. Then he looked at Andry with a bright smile and beckoned for him to sit near him.

"We don't have much time, Andry." It was the first time he had called him by name. Andry understood: this was important, listen up! "You're bursting with questions, I know. But I must ask first. You know of Vasyllia, yes?" Andry nodded. "I thought you would. Old stock, here. But have you heard of the Deathless?"

Andry's skin crawled. The old terror at the edge of light and dark. The Deathless was the great evil that had been chained to the pit of the earth by Voran the Warrior, thousands of years ago.

He nodded, but he avoided the old man's eyes.

"Did you know there are prophecies that the Deathless, or at least his evil, will eventually return? Some of them speak of the coming of a son to the Deathless one, a foul spawn of dark magic and unclean ritual?"

Andry didn't understand those words. But his twisting gut confirmed that they were nothing good.

"There are those, Andry, who would bring an entire generation of sons, not just one son of the Deathless, into the world by force."

"Not you?" Such a thing seemed too horrible to be possible.

Apsat looked at Andry for a long moment. Andry hoped with all the strength of his body and soul that the old man would not says yes.

Apsat shook his head. Andry remembered to breathe.

"But why?" he asked, and immediately felt embarrassed. His mother was always telling him to stop asking that question. He kept forgetting.

"The old things, Andry. Power. Lust. Desire for control. They will tell you that all they want is an end to the war that has taken so many innocent lives. They might even believe it, at that."

He was speaking to himself again, his gaze internal. Andry remained quiet, still, hoping the old man would continue talking that way. It was more interesting than when he spoke to him as a child.

"There is no way out of this that preserves you as you are, Dunai," he droned, almost like a drunk. "Perhaps it is best that you kill me now."

Suddenly the trees all groaned from a gust of wind that came from nowhere, bending all of them halfway to the earth. One or two of the old maples cracked in half. Andry jumped up. Apsat closed his eyes and stayed in place.

Three huge white wolves crept toward them from the woods opposite the wheat fields. Their growls were so loud they rumbled inside Andry's chest.

Apsat nodded and extended his arms.

"Dunai, hear me first. I am your midwife, not your murderer.

If you will trust, as you have never had reason to trust, I believe that you will have what you most desire."

Something strange happened inside Andry. He felt words forming inside him, but they weren't his. And yet they were. It was very confusing. He thought them, but the voice of that thought was a woman's. It said, "You cannot give me what I want. You are only a man."

Apsat bowed his head. He answered as though he had heard the voice inside Andry. "And yet, like you, I move people and events. Subtly. Clearing out the underbrush. Making a path clear for new growth."

The wolves stopped.

"If you can arrange it...will I survive?" asked Dunai in Andry's heart.

Apsat didn't answer. He did not have an answer.

The wolves retreated, and the trees stood straight again. Birdsong resumed, the sun cleared a bank of clouds, and warmth washed over Andry's face.

"I'm sorry, Andry," said Apsat, and his eyes were heavy with pain. "You are a special boy. You deserve a long life of peace in the Dunaian way. But none of us choose the days in which we are born."

"The war is coming here, isn't it?" asked Andry.

Apsat nodded.

§

THE YOUNG SOLDIER was waiting for them, his body seeming to lounge under the eaves of Yan's hut as he sucked on a dandelion stem. But Andry could tell that his pose was that of a hunting cat pretending not to see its prey.

Irena stood by him silently, her eyes drinking him in, her fingers absently playing with the end of her braid. She was whispering something private to the young man. He chuckled, but didn't look back at her, studiously avoiding her gaze. It made her look at him even more longingly.

Father and Mother puttered about the garden, seemingly hard at work, but Andry saw they were just going through the motions.

The soldier saw Apsat, and his body went rigid. There was a clear challenge in his eyes as he stared at his older counterpart.

Apsat nodded, and the young man smiled. It was a vulpine smile. He took Irena's hand suddenly and kissed the tips of her fingers, then dropped her hand, but tenderly. Irena's face went bright red, but her smile was knowing.

Andry's world had changed forever, he knew that now. Nothing would ever be the same.

"My friends," said Apsat, "we have presumed on your hospitality long enough. It is time we go."

The last sentence was said insistently at the young soldier, with an edge of warning. The young soldier smiled without his eyes and did something with his fingers. A twisting motion.

Apsat's face went white. He mouthed a silent "No!"

Something shifted in the air, like a sudden absence of wind in the middle of a snowstorm. One moment, it was a typical spring day in Dunai. The next, the air throbbed with what looked like golden dust flying around like murmurations of starlings. It was everywhere. They were breathing it in and breathing it out. It was in their eyes, though they could not sense it. Andry caressed it with his fingers, and it twisted like eddies of water around him. He felt nothing; it was too fine.

"What is it?" asked Irena, mesmerized. "It's so beautiful."

The young man laughed, and for a moment, there was genuine enjoyment in his face.

"You poor fools," he said. "Surrounded by living gold, the wealth of entire nations at your feet, and you do nothing with it! Just eat and sleep and die like the rest of us."

"Budzislav, be silent!" commanded Apsat.

But the young soldier only sneered at him. "Why? Shouldn't

these people know why they're about to lose everything? Wouldn't that be the kind thing to do?"

"Lose everything? What do you mean?" asked Papa.

Apsat sighed and put his hand out to silence Budzislav, but the young man didn't pay any attention.

"The acanthia flower. It is not a flower. It is the fruiting body of a something like a very large mushroom. And these are its spores." He pointed at the gold dust, then twisted his hand again, and the dust disappeared. "Everywhere present, filling all, and completely invisible." This last felt like an incantation or a ritual address. It sounded strange coming from his cynical face.

"Why is that important?" Mother's face looked like it was whitewashed.

"The Dunai, not just your village, but the entire region," began Apsat, unwillingly, "it is integrated with a massive living creature. Something like a root system, but belonging to a single being, similar to a mushroom's mycelium. It is the reason that all the growing things here *help* each other thrive. The reason that all the living things seem connected to each other. They are indeed connected through the spores that permeate everything. *You* are all connected as well. To the largest creature ever to live on the realm of Earth. Its edges are the edges of Dunai. Its heart is the heart of this realm. It *is* Dunai."

"Don't dance around it, Apsat. Tell them!" Budzislav seemed now to be the commander, not the young upstart.

Apsat sighed, but complied.

"Many ages ago, when Voran the Warrior defeated the Deathless, a part of Vasyllia was raised, physically, into the realm of Aer. It is said that those who die in sacrifice to their fellows go to that place after death to live eternally in peace. A blessed realm of plenty. I don't know the truth of it. But it has long been believed by the wise that some of the water that flows from the peaks of Vasyllia is... alive. Life-giving. Healing."

"Oh, for the Hart's sake," Budzislav interrupted. "There is living water in the soil of Dunai. It has come from that land in the mountains, Vasyllia as was. And Dunai, the *land* itself, has come alive. You're living on ground that is awake. Sentient. Alive. Do you understand what that means?"

Papa laughed, but it was a black thing, clanking in Andry's ears. "We understand better than you ever could. You intend to use it. For the war."

"Think of it!" Budzislav sounded like a madman. "Endless food sources for our armies, food that is nourishing like no other. A new crop of young warriors from the Dunai, stronger than all other men. Water that not only quenches thirst, but gives physical strength in the middle of a battle. Think of it!"

"You're lying," said Mama, her hands shaking. "Do you think we're stupid? I didn't know it until now, but I have no doubt. You serve the priestess of Kosh. You are a black magician. There is something here, in the life of this land, that you need for your magic. What is it? Some kind of weapon? Something that will devastate the enemy once and for all?"

Although Budzislav visibly bristled when Mama said "priestess of Kosh," he made a visible effort to calm himself. Then he inclined his head, like a swordsman acknowledging a good strike. "Something like that, yes."

"Shame!" cried Mama. "To use a source of life to sow death among your enemies."

"You put it well, matron," said Budzislav, but he was done talking. "Are you coming, Apsat, or should I tell our lady that you have finally gone native?"

Andry felt the prickly threat of those words.

Apsat and Budzislav stared at each other for long seconds, both their bodies tense, ready for action. Apsat was the first to deflate, his head falling on his chest.

"I'm ready," he said. To Andry, still standing at his right, he turned and kneeled. He took both his shoulders in his hands and stared at him directly in the eyes. The old soldier's deep-green eyes were canny, kind, but terrible too. Andry forced himself not to look away.

"Andry, you are connected to the land like no one else," he whispered so that no one would hear. "You were born on a purple morning. You can see the lady, in a way that no one else can. These things are not accidents. Seek Dunai's strength. You will need it."

Andry wanted to kiss the old man and hug him, but he felt it would be the wrong thing to do.

"Vohin Apsat," he whispered. "Why does that young man have power over you?"

Apsat's eyes widened in surprise.

"He serves someone. Someone very bad. And my family is in danger."

Andry nodded, his mouth firming. He wanted to help Apsat. But how?

CHAPTER

SIX

THE NEW WORLD

ndry had been right. Nothing was the same after Apsat
and Budzislav left.

It started more quickly than he expected. A morning
only a week afterward, Andry woke up to Mama's shrieks and
Papa's pointless attempts to smother them with his bear hug.

It was Irena. She had run away, leaving only a note.

*I'm going to my love. He is the future, and I want to be there with him
for it. You will never understand.*

That was it. Andry didn't understand, but he felt Mama's pain,
huge and horrible as it was.

The house went quiet and tense after that, and it never came
back to normal.

The reason was simple. About a month later, as the early
summer's heat was just becoming prickly on the skin and Andry
could think of nothing from morning to night except jumping
into water and staying there for hours, the first caravan of soldiers
appeared.

They came in rows of four, with silver helmets ringed with fur,
with a single plume above the brow-ridge. Most soldiers were

spear-bearers with swords and odd round shields on their hips, wearing old mail that barely covered their clothes of simple linen and leather. But a few were mounted knights with plate mail chest and shoulder plates. These had strange banners tied to their backs that looked like swan's wings, made of what looked like real white feathers. Behind them rode banner-bearers carrying square flags of pure sable with a silver sun in the middle, surrounded by five stars. Andry thought the stars might actually be made of diamond or some other precious gem, they shone so brightly in the sun.

It was still two months before harvest festival. And they didn't act like soldiers coming to harvest festival. They acted like lords come into an inheritance.

One morning, Andry watched a group of them from his window, standing before Otar Kalavan as he talked to them in his soft, firm way. Andry didn't hear his words, but their faces made it clear they were hardly listening. Before he had even finished, one of them pushed Otar Kalavan to the side, and the priest fell over his own feet. Andry gasped, but the soldiers laughed. One of them spit on the priest's cassock.

It got worse. Mama refused to let Kira or Aglusha out without Papa in tow. Aglusha punched pillows more often than before, but Kira took it without complaint. She tried to avoid any errands that would take her outside the house. In the evenings, she would sit by the hearth with hollow eyes and cry, trying not to look at anyone.

In the evening, Andry heard his parents whisper that the soldiers had attacked Elania in the streets. Andry's chest burned with fury and terror both. He wanted to do something, but had no idea what that might be. Things like this never had happened to anyone in Dunai before.

The merchants came next. They were Gruzinans for the most part, with their long beards, coffee-scented aromas, and wide pantaloons, and so were not an unusual sight in Dunai. What was unusual was that they all came with empty carts. They had never before come with carts that failed to be overflowing with metal-work marvels, bunches of silks, and bags of coffee and saffron. But these merchants were not here to trade. They were here to take.

As soon as the early squashes, peas, and root vegetables came into their own, the soldiers forced the Dunaians at sword point—young women, children, even the old cripples in the common house—to gather everything and pile it all indiscriminately on the carts of the merchants, who only sat around and made jokes to each other that Andry didn't understand. They never made eye contact with the Dunaians, even though Andry knew many of them by first name from previous harvest festivals.

More and more soldiers came, and the fields sprouted trian-gular tents, topped with flapping banners bearing that sigil of the silver sun and five stars.

The worst was that the Dunaians seemed incapable of doing anything to stop it. They seemed more bewildered than anything. Even when the young men began to be stopped in the streets and taken at spear-point to the pavilions in the field, no one did anything. When word got around that they were being impressed into Karila's armies for the forever-war, the women cried and the children's faces went pale.

But no one *did* anything.

Then the groves of trees came down by the tens to make room for the multiplying pavilions, and the most anyone did was glare at the soldiers.

Finally, the hunting began. Cries of dying birds, deer, bison, and boar filled the air. Birdsong stopped entirely. The silence between the dying screeches were even worse, because Andry kept waiting for a new one to begin.

Huge metal canisters on legs like overgrown bugs were shoved into the ground on the edges of the village. Stacks of black smoke rose from them. The smell coming from them, though, was the worst part for Andry. Because he couldn't help it: the smell of smoked meat made his mouth water. He felt dirty just for thinking about it.

And still, no one did anything. No one said anything.

No one, that is, except Pitirim.

Andry hardly recognized the old man. He was just as grubby and feeble-looking as ever, his scrawny knees perpetually knocking against each other as he walked. But his voice seemed to have gathered the strength of ten as he walked through the crowds of lounging soldiers, beating their mailed shoulders with his feeble fists. The soldiers didn't know what to do with him. Whether it was a glamour of compassion, bewilderment, or something more magical, no one raised a hand against him, not matter how wild his antics.

One day it was Pitirim walking with a bucket of mud in one hand, and the priest's hyssop in another. He intoned nonsense syllables as he pretended to lead a ritual procession. But instead of using the hyssop reed to sprinkle water of sanctification, he rained mud on the faces of the soldiers. As he did, he cried out things like "Receive the bounty of your labors!" and "Be blessed with the fruit of your deeds!" The soldiers recoiled as the mud flew, but most laughed at him.

Another day he ran through them screaming at the top of his lungs, interrupting his cries with a single phrase, "The mother has the sharpest teeth of all!" Then he squatted with his arms outstretched, fingers splayed, and pulled his neck out long like a turkey's. He squawked and waddled around like a chicken.

Another day he hid behind the houses and flung flowers at passing soldiers. "Watch out!" He said as they passed. "They'll get you in the end!"

But the soldiers and merchants weren't the only targets for Pitirim's madness. He attacked the men of Dunai even more fiercely. One day he went so far as to hurl still-bloody chicken innards at a group of young men who huddled by the fires of the storyteller's pit, talking in hushed voices to each other.

"Little chickens got more guts'n you!" He squawked at them.

Andry loved the old man more and more.

And then the rumors started.

"Goran sold Elania to the highest bidder," said Papa one evening to Mama, when he thought the children were asleep. "Got some paper promising he and his wife would be protected when the war starts."

Mama's face turned dark red with fury. "Rumors," she said. "Filthy rumors."

"I hope you're right," Yan said, too tired to argue.

But Andry no longer saw Elania in the streets, nor did her eyes sparkle in the windows as he passed the smithy.

The rumor was confirmed for Andry when Pitirim tripped Goran in the streets as the smith was passing by. As the large man fell, Pitirim overturned a pail of rotten vegetables on his head.

"Be safe," he said, and for a moment the playful demeanor fell off his face, and Andry was looking at the eyes of someone who understood power. Goran shriveled before that look.

Then Pitirim smiled his idiot smile and pranced away as though nothing had happened. Goran wept openly, not even trying to clean his head and face from the stinking goop.

As the antics got more and more insane, a few of the soldiers began to grumble whenever Pitirim appeared. Some began to puff their chests out and not give way if he tried to walk past them as they had before. Some began to stick out their feet as he ran past them, trying to trip him. Some of the Dunaians did as well. But Pitirim was like a goat. He just hopped around them and never seemed to trip unless he fell on purpose, as he did once, dramatically flinging himself into a puddle of rainwater and crying out, "Oh, how clean this water is! As pure as the priestess's love!"

That got him a barked command or two, which he cheerfully pretended not to hear.

Andry felt the charged atmosphere in the village get worse by the day, and he knew the soldiers would soon hurt Pitirim if he didn't stop.

One evening, when the late spring rain got heavy and unpleasant enough for the soldiers to mostly retreat into the relative comfort of their tents, Andry slipped out of the house as the rest of the household was hard at work shucking peas. He had been pretending to read, and Mama was so pleased, she was studiously trying not to look in his general direction. It was the perfect chance, and he took it.

He slunk from tree to tree, avoiding the village roads, trying to find Pitirim. He wasn't in any of his usual places. It took Andry so long that he began to feel soldiers lurking behind him at every step. But there was no one around. All the houses' wall-stoves were happily puffing away, and not even a stray animal passed near Andry. He hardly felt the presence of any living thing near him. That, more than anything, added to the fear scratching at the back of his neck.

Finally, he had an insight, bright and single.

He ran up the hill to the place where Apsat had shown him the mountain beyond the mountain, where old Vasyllia itself hid somewhere up in the clouds.

Standing in a clearing, the rain pouring off him as though he was the source of it, Pitirim looked up at the mountain and wept so fiercely that Andry saw the tears falling in spite of the rain. He had a look in his eyes that Andry had never seen in anyone. Some combination of pain and love and hope and despair. It was an impossible look with too much in it—too much for any person.

"Pitirim, you're going to get yourself killed," said Andry, putting a hand on his outstretched right arm.

"I certainly hope so," said Pitirim, more clearly than Andry had ever heard him speak. "Maybe then they'll wake up from their sleeping."

"You mean us?"

"Not you, little fire-sprite," he said. His smile was fatherly, lighting a warmth in Andry's belly.

"Pitirim, do you think..." but he dared not say what had been nagging him at the back of his thoughts throughout these weeks as he watched his world fall apart.

"Say it, boy." For a moment, he sounded like Apsat.

"This is a punishment, isn't it? For not being worthy of Dunai."

Pitirim sighed deeply, and his face contracted into a grimace of weeping that was almost comical in its intensity.

"Humans are more than just animals," he said. "If we were not, then Dunai would be for us. But we are more. And we are also much, much less."

Andry waited, trying not to move, even as the rain tickled his nose terribly.

"I hoped. I wanted to believe. Never, not in the history of the Three Lands, has there been a place like Dunai. I had hoped it would be the start of something new. A refuge you could actually reach."

He looked back up at the mountain, and this time there was a look of reproach. He even seemed about to shake his fist at the mountain. But he didn't.

"It seems that we human beings cannot exist in a place like Dunai without it rotting us from within. We need... difficulties. Grist. Whetstones. Without it... well, you can see it."

Andry's chest was tight, like someone was hugging him too hard.

"What are we going to do?"

"We?" Pitirim's laughter was grim. "There is no 'we' in Dunai, it seems."

He turned and walked back into the forest and down into the village.

Andry wanted to scream, he was so frustrated. Instead, he kept it inside. He looked at the distant mountain range, too high to be possible, that he had only seen for the first time with Apsat. If it was there, it was wreathed in fog and mist. All he thought he saw was a vague shape of something mountain-like. But it could have been a trick of the mist.

EITHER PITIRIM WAS FASTER than his knock-kneed appearance suggested, or Andry had stood there, looking for the mountain of Old Vasyllia, far longer than he realized. He couldn't see where Pitirim had gone. Not that it should matter: the old man went wherever he wanted, whenever he wanted.

But Andry's heart twinged—something was wrong. He stopped halfway down the hill path in mid stride. Was that the sound of metal scraping against metal?

At his right, a nuthatch called its brash *chirr-RUP!* Over his head, two black squirrels screeched at each other, fighting over a nut. A cloud of mayflies descended on Andry, faintly wheezing just on the edge of hearing.

But no sound of metal on metal.

Then, someone screamed.

It was to Andry's left. Without thinking, he plunged into the underbrush, immediately denting his shin against an old log that still had some bite to its bark. The pain lanced up his leg, then dimmed to a buzz. Andry ran on.

Laughter, harsh like the clatter of stones falling down a cliff. At least three different sources of laughter, though all three had a similar ring. Like they were three manifestations of the same evil. A smell, sharp like musk, invaded Andry's nose.

Just downhill of Andry, Pitirim was on his knees, his hands covering his head. Surrounding him from three sides were Karilan soldiers, fully armed, all holding maces with spikes like long thorns. One of the maces dripped blood.

"No!" Andry was screaming before his mind caught up with his mouth.

A second mace came down and shattered Pitirim's face. Or that's what it sounded like—Andry couldn't see from behind.

"No!" Andry's legs were moving faster than he had thought possible, even though everything else seemed to be moving at a snail's pace, including...

... the third mace, lodging itself in the back of Pitirim's head with a dull thud and staying there.

"NO!" Andry's scream echoed, reverberated, as though the trees were picking up the sound and tossing it from branch to branch.

One of the soldiers saw him. He raised his mace and swung it down. It was a wild swing, badly aimed. It missed Andry's head. But it bit into his shoulder, then tore. Andry felt the skin cleave and the thorns of the mace-head gouge him. Something hot splashed his face. He fell, and things started to spin around him. The soldier raised the mace again. His eyes were hungry, like the wolves' that had come for Apsat before Dunai had changed her mind.

Dunai's presence filled his mind. He couldn't see her, not quite. But it was like she inhabited every cranny of his peripheral vision with her huge warmth and darkness. Silently, he cried out to her.

Help.

All three soldiers froze in place at the same time, though in Andry's eyes they seemed to spin around still. Their eyes turned white and huge from fear.

There was buzzing in the air so thick that Andry felt it like a wave rolling over his body.

The soldiers screamed and writhed, their hands clutching their faces, scratching at them until the blood seeped between their fingers.

They were covered in seething masses of bees—big, furry ones —from head to foot. Their screaming was like pigs being slaughtered. Andry felt sick at the sound.

All at once, as if they were a single person in three bodies, the soldiers slumped to the ground. The earth parted around their prone forms and swallowed them into the soft leafmold.

Andry closed his eyes. His mind was confused, and he kept seeing strange colors in the corner of his closed eyelids.

He had a strange thought.

Dunai! Choose Pitirim.

But that was the last thought he had before his closed eyes filled with a light so bright, the inside of his eyelids turned pink. And then, he remembered no more.

CHAPTER
SEVEN

THE MOTHER OF KISH

ndry sat on a hillock outside town, the morning sun of late summer a pleasant tickle on his back. His fingers absently played with the faded-green grass and the blue chicory flowers that heralded the shortening of the days. He breathed deeply, trying to push out the pain in his chest that grabbed like a hook between his rib bones. It caught and tweaked him as he breathed, making him twitch. Smells of roast pork filled his nostrils. He tried to cough them out. It didn't work.

He pulled at the grass in frustration, breaking each blade individually, carefully, from its proper patch.

This was the worst part of the death of Andry's world. Dunai had chosen him instead of Pitirim, letting the old man die, then taking him into the same grave as the three soldiers who had killed him. He had been delirious for days after that, and still, his mind had odd blanks when he lost entire minutes at a time.

But the worst wasn't the physical effects. He had lost any connection with Dunai.

It was as if the lady of the land were angry with him for making her choose. The animals no longer whispered to him. People's thoughts were once again blank, their faces not turned toward him at all. The grass was just grass. The trees were nothing more than trees, no longer little worlds filled with small lives and minuscule, simple joys.

As Andry tugged at one of the blades of grass, his finger slipped, and he nicked it. The pain was sharp, sudden. He looked at the red welling up in his finger, and he sucked the saltiness away.

The pain and the taste of salt cleared his mind like nothing had for weeks.

He realized he had been a fool. No, Dunai wasn't angry.

He turned around to look back at the village, the tenseness in the air now something different that it had been before. Was there something odd about the movements of the soldiers? Yes, now that he focused on it, it was clear as day. From his vantage point, he saw the central square laid out like a game board before him, with three of the main roads leading into the flagstone-tiled square that wasn't so much a square as an irregular rhombus. The shape had the effect of drawing the eye toward the tallest building in the village: the church.

All three of the roads, he saw now as though for the first time, entered the square so that the first thing anyone saw was the spire with its onion-domed bell tower, its twelve bells open to sky and sight. Two of the roads wove through the rickety stalls of the marketplace, which had been shuttered for weeks. One was a straight line going through the alley with the bookbinder's, smithy, bakery, and other larger establishments.

At the beginning of this strangest of summers, Andry had seen hardly anything but soldiers in those roads and in the square strutting, laughing, their mail shining in the sun.

But now he realized they had been skulking in twos and threes for weeks, some of them avoiding even their own kind. He watched it play out right in front of him: as a pair entered the square, they unconsciously turned away from the church. That was interesting, though Andry didn't understand why that should be.

The merchants were conspicuously absent as well.

Of course!

He had been an idiot. The merchants hadn't been around much at all, lately. Even Kira had noted it over dinner in a rare moment when she took a break from crying silently by the hearth. Mama had smiled bitterly, and Papa had sighed. He was sighing a lot these days.

Andry hadn't paid it much heed at the time. One of his blank-nesses had occurred then, and he was confused for a time. Now, it made sense. The merchants were not around because they had left. And they had left because the land was not producing as much food as they had been promised. They had plenty of busi-ness in other lands, why waste it on a false paradise?

So why had the land stopped producing food?

If only Dunai would talk to Andry. If she was anything like the people of her land, she should be pining for the companionable harmony between humans and animals and growing things that she always fostered. That constant hum of common life that had gone silent. She had to know that Andry would listen to her, even if she just wanted to complain.

He closed his eyes and tried to see her, like he had done before. But nothing happened. He hadn't seen an acanthia flower anywhere for weeks.

Dunai was intent on avoiding him, it seemed.

He turned around, his back to the village, staring out into the wide world that had never before held any attraction for him.

Something shimmered in the distance on the single road leading into Dunai. The sea of pavilions in front of him shud-dered into movement as tent flaps flew open. People rushed about, seething like those strange insects that had covered the dead goldfinch. Everywhere, the glint of mail, but more than that, a sharper glint here and there, like fireflies in the corner of your eye. Drawn swords, upraised spears, axes and adzes brandished.

Something was happening. And it did not bode well.

Now he was sure: someone was approaching the village. Someone ridiculously huge, impossibly huge.

He sat frozen in place as the thing came closer and closer into focus, even as his mind was telling him to run away, to flee, to dig a burrow into the ground and stay there until the danger passed.

The more he saw the thing, the less possible it seemed. Once, when he was very little, he had heard Mama tell a story of Prince Illan and the fire-maned horse. He had loved that story, but Aglusha's world had been turned around by it. That horse, for her, became the only thing she thought about, talked about, dreamed about. She even drew it, and Aglusha was terrible at drawing. Not surprisingly, the horse turned out all wrong. It was the size of a house, with legs like tree trunks and a mane that looked like overgrown ears. Andry had laughed at it, but now he thought maybe his silly sister had prophetic powers.

Because that fire-maned horse of her imagination was walking directly toward Dunai.

The size of a house, legs like tree trunks, but it was the wrong color. Its skin was something between grey and brown, textured like sandstone. It didn't have a mane, but the ears were massive like triangular banners flapping in the wind. And the biggest difference was the face. It had a tail on its face.

As Andry was trying to put together the strange bits of that creature into something he could understand, the tail on its face twisted like a snake rearing its head, and it blatted a sound like an oxhorn echoing in a narrow gorge. Under that rearing snake was a small mouth with two huge metal-tipped tusks.

And then he saw that the creature had a saddle on its back, almost like a small house itself, with sheer curtains edged in gold thread on all four sides. Inside sat a figure with long, curling hair barely silhouetted against the sun. He felt, more than saw, the intensity of that figure's eyes.

Astonishment fought with terror inside Andry, until a feather-light touch at the edge of his hearing distracted him. Dunai. She had reached out to him. She needed him.

Finally.

That was enough to break him from his frozen posture. He ran home as quickly as he could, knowing that the summons—whatever they were, in what form he couldn't imagine—would come soon enough.

❧

THEY CAME that evening in the form of Budzislav himself.

He knocked at the door, and Papa opened it. When Mama saw who it was, she shrieked and seemed about to attack the young soldier. Papa did something Andry never saw him do. He barked at Mama to stop. Andry's blood chilled at the sound. But Budzislav's cold smile was even worse.

"She's doing well, before you ask," said Budzislav, making as if to enter the house. Papa stood in his way, forcing Andry to change seats. He needed to see how this would end.

"Say your piece," rumbled Yan, still seething with that never-before-seen fury. "And leave quickly. Desperate men cannot be relied on."

Andry assumed Papa meant Budzislav, but the young soldier's expression made it clear that Papa was talking about himself.

"The Mother of Kish has come in person, as you no doubt already know. She wishes to speak to the heads of all the Dunai families tomorrow morning at first bell. In the town square."

"I will be there," said Yan, and began to close the door in Budzislav's face.

"Oh, and..." Budzislav put his mailed hand on the door and held it in place. "Bring the boy. Apsat wants to see him."

❧

WHEN ANDRY WALKED with his father to the village square the next morning, they went the long way. Instead of taking the twisty alleys, where clotheslines hung like old cobwebs, to the pitted stone road through the artisan's quarter, Yan led them along the straight, muddy road through the shuttered stalls of the market place, a place that had always been the beating heart of the village.

Now, even the puddles of fetid water looked lonely. Yan stopped before each of the stalls and stared for a moment, as though he were trying to remember something important. Or maybe it was to memorize the details of this day. Andry understood. This was going to be the most important day of their lives.

They entered the square and stopped dead in their tracks. It wasn't the oddly pristine lines of Dunaian farmers and tradesmen and artisans standing at almost military attention. It wasn't the ring of helmeted spear-bearers standing at elbow-length intervals all along the outer edge of the square. It was the fact that you couldn't see the church. Or rather, that something else, much greater, stood in front of it.

Now that Andry saw it up close, it was no longer terrifying. Aglusha's horse-like-a-house was exotic for sure, but it was still an animal, a creature that Andry couldn't help but want to know better. It had small, beady eyes that looked exhausted and even seemed to have a rheumy edge to them, like it was physically ill from its long journey. The tail on its face wasn't a tail at all. It was a very long nose. The silliness of the sight made Andry want to laugh with pleasure.

But then he saw that the pavilion on top of the great animal was open to the air. The drapes had been removed, revealing an absurdly out-of-place chair that blazed with gold in the summer sunlight. On that chair was the most beautiful woman Andry had ever seen.

She wasn't exotic in her beauty. There was nothing storybook about her. No "sable-edged eyebrows" or "hair like flowing gold" or "eyes blazing like diamonds" or any of the other repeated phrases from the old tales. But everyone's eyes were riveted to nowhere but her face. It was perfectly symmetrical. Andry had never seen a face like it.

Like most Karilan women, she wore a beaded headscarf. But she didn't have it tied in the proper manner. Rather, it was loose, untied, allowing curling brown hair to frame her face pleasantly. Her close-fitting tunic was many-colored, bright, but not garish. Over it, she wore loose saffron-colored robes that softened what otherwise would have been an angular, almost masculine figure. Her eyes were dirt-brown, unimpressive at first, until they looked at Andry. When they did, he had a feeling that this woman cared for the whole world like it was her own child. She was a mother to everyone. A mother to the whole world.

That thought terrified him, though he couldn't understand why, or whether it was his own thought, or the thought of Dunai permeating him.

At the feet of the great beast was an honor guard of black-skinned warriors larger than any men Andry had seen. To his own surprise, he hazily remembered a tale of a kingdom far beyond the sands of the Eastern Desert that was famed for its warriors and its wise men. He felt a thrill of excitement.

Among them, closest to the legs of the beast, stood Budzislav and Apsat, his kestrel sitting on his left shoulder. It seemed to be staring into Andry's eyes directly, fluttering with the pleasure of seeing a familiar face.

It was a very human gesture.

The Mother of Kish stood up inside her pavilion, even though to Andry it seemed dangerous to stand on the back of a beast whose single step would cause her to tumble to the red brick cobbles of the square in a moment. She seemed not in the least afraid of that happening, as was clear from every movement of her body. She looked like a dancer, completely confident of every twitch of a finger, every curve of an eyebrow.

It was mesmerizing. So mesmerizing, in fact, that Andry missed the beginning of her speech. He hurried to force his mind to the words.

"...taken from the earth by force. Not by my blessing, I assure you. And the punishment, believe me, will be intense. How intense may depend on you, fine people."

Andry was confused. She was speaking like a mediator in a quarrel between two sides at war. As though she were not the cause of everything horrible that had already happened. Surely no one would believe that to be true. Did she think Dunaians were stupid?

"I seek not your forced submission, but an alliance. I have a signed charter to speak on behalf of the Shuudanate of the Karilan Protectorate. I am, as it were, the mouth of the Shuudan."

Her lips curled at this, as though she had made a joke. But Andry would never call that face-twisting a smile. Neither did he understand why it should be a joke. The empress of Karila was no laughing matter, especially not the current empress, judging by the conversations of his parents.

"My lady," said Papa, to Andry's surprise. "Speak plainly, please. We Dunaians are not canny courtiers who enjoy twistings in words and hidden meanings behind insinuations. We are folk of the earth. We say what we mean and do what we intend. What do you want of us that you have not already taken by force?"

A slight pursing of the lips, a flash of added color to her cheeks—both quickly overcome by an obvious force of will. If Andry had thought Apsat dangerous once, he realized that compared to this woman, Apsat was a lapdog with a lolling tongue.

"Yes, I had forgotten about your blunt manners," she said to Papa, but meant it for all the assembled. "Very well, it shall be as you wish."

She snapped her fingers, and one of the tall black-skinned warriors unrolled a brown paper that had been scrolled into a tube. He had a strange accent that was pleasant to listen to. Andry imagined he had a wonderful singing voice.

"By order of the Shuudan (may the Hart bless her for all her days), the Mother of Kish, supreme priestess of the Hart, is given the ancestral lands of Dunai as a gift for her service to the Protectorate and her many labors in the war against Nebesta's rebellious sons. She may do with these lands as she sees fit. It is the wish of the Protectorate that these lands, rich in lore and in the earth's bounty, may serve not merely her pleasure, but the needs of us all. Signed, Alatava the Ninth, Shuudan of the Grand Protectorate of the Karila."

The buzzing in the crowd started at the first sentence and turned into a burbling just on the brink of shouting by the end.

The Mother of Kish smiled at them all, and Andry couldn't help feeling she was the only reasonable one in the crowd. But that thought felt twisted... wrong... not quite his own.

Budzislav waved a hand over the crowd, and the sounds faded as silent mouths continued to flap open and shut, like fish trying to breathe air. That powerful bit of magic, effortlessly cast over them all, stilled everyone.

The Mother of Kish nodded once, pleased.

"This is what the Shuudan has given, in her bounty. But I have come here to tell you that I will not take this gift of the Shuudan unless *you* wish me to."

Papa guffawed. Andry froze into terrified stillness at that sound. Did he want to get killed on the spot?

"And if we do not wish it, what?" Papa shouted at her, not even trying to be civil. "You will take all your armies and leave us alone?"

She looked directly at Papa, then, to Andry's horror, she looked at Andry for a very long time, as though she were searching for something inside his head. He felt that his body would betray him at any moment and run away.

But she looked away at the exact moment he was about to bolt.

"That is exactly what I will do, yes."

That caused another stir.

"Hear me, fine people of Dunai. You need not make any hasty judgments. I will be fully honest with you."

She extended her hands out before her, palms-down, as though balancing her body on the edge of a precipice. Then she stepped off the beast... onto thin air.

She floated down like a leaf in a calm glade.

Andry looked at Budzislav as she descended. His body was shaking with physical strain. There was a clear line of sweat on his brow. So the magic was his—that was interesting. Andry wondered if the Mother of Kish had any magic of her own, or if she simply used Budzislav and Apsat as her two hands.

She stood at the foot of the great beast, in front of the line of warrior-guards. Andry was surprised to see how small she was.

"People of Dunai. You do not know this yet. And I do not blame you if you find it hard to believe. But we are here to protect you."

Half the men laughed out loud. The other half looked ready to burst with the effort of not laughing. To Andry's surprise, the Mother of Kish did not seem to take offense.

"You have been cut off from the larger world. You do not know that the Nebesti guerrillas have grown stronger over the years. That they have sought, and found, allies in distant lands you may have not heard of. That there is, at this very moment, an allied army of Nebesti and Gruzinans and mercenaries from the distant East, fell wolf-riders whose ancestors mixed with dark creatures of the forest, befouling their blood. This army is, even now, coming to take Dunai and its bounty for themselves."

The laughter died. Her manner was so sincere, so much like a concerned mother, that it was difficult to do anything but believe her.

"Dunaians! Don't you realize that your idyll is over? You have had this little paradise to yourselves now for centuries. For centuries, the peoples of all lands have come to your autumn festival in peace. And no one ever thought anything of it, except that perhaps there was something special about the soil in these lands. An unusually fruitful country. Not unheard of in the past, certainly."

Everything she said was true. But Andry didn't like the color of it. It felt vaguely like *they* were at fault for hoarding the riches of Dunai. Which was absurd. Or was it?

"But something happened at some point in your past. A hundred years ago? Fifty? *Ten*, perhaps?"

And she looked at Andry again. The chills shimmied down his back from his neck to his toes. This was not good at all. What was she saying?

"Yes, I believe it was something like ten years ago. Something happened—who knows what?—but the land began to give even more. The harvests became not merely bountiful, but they seemed to respond to the specific needs of that year. You know of what I speak, yes? Perhaps there was a year when a granary filled with—oh, lets's say, oats?—was lost in a fire. I believe that did happen a few years back..."

It had. Andy remembered it like a half-dream from his early childhood. It had been his family's granary.

"And the following year had an absurd harvest of oats, is not that true?"

Half the men in the square were nodding, most of them with the kind of half-fear, half-exhilaration that comes from a terrible realization.

"Or perhaps one year there was an unusual winter sickness. I know you rarely get them here, but perhaps there was a year when half the children were on the verge of death after a sickness that drained them of their bodies's weight and left them like skeletons?"

Andry remembered. It was two year ago. Aglusha had gotten sick, along with most of the children in the village. It had been a shocking thing, considering hardly anyone ever got sick here. In Dunai, even the old people simply died in their sleep, calmly. But during that winter of sickness, the animals had started to come daily, in groups of two and three, to die on the edges of the village and offer their meat to the Dunaian children. Mama had said that it was the meat that had strengthened Aglusha enough for her to survive the sickness as it passed through the village.

"And then... it all stopped, did it not?"

The murmurs began again.

"And yet, the land has not provided for you this growing season. You have seen it even in the herb gardens behind your houses, have you not? The stunted growth, the lack of rain, the way the ground has turned sandy in places, as though all the water had been drained of it from inside? You blame my soldiers for this, do you not?"

"Well, what else could it be?" Papa challenged her. Andry noticed none of the other men turned to look at him as he spoke. Another bad sign. "They came, and the land stopped giving. It seems quite simple."

"But is that true, Yan of the Dunai?" She mocked him gently, still like a mother. "Was not the land giving its bounty in even greater profusion for the first month of the occupation?"

Andry wondered why *she* was calling it an occupation. Wasn't she the one who had ordered it? She was playing some kind of dangerous game.

"Was there not a day, nay, even a specific moment, when the land turned in on itself, stopped giving to invader and Dunaian alike?"

A few of the men turned to look at Papa. No, not at Papa. At *him*. Why?

"Can it possibly be you have not wondered at why this should have happened?"

They were now *all* looking at him. All except Papa. What was going on?

The silence was immense. Andry felt it as a silence not only of the people, but of all the birds, animals, even the earth itself. A terror like a huge, toothed mouth seemed to hang over him. His heart raced so fast he started to go dizzy.

"Tell them, Yan of the Dunai. Tell *him*. Tell him the truth."

"He's a child!" Yan screamed. "He's only a child!"

73

"Not *only*," said the Mother of Kish, her voice lowering dangerously. "He was born on a purple morning. And not just born. Born outside, under the open sky, in a circle of acanthia flowers..."

She ended the sentence as though she was planning to continue, but had stopped herself at the last moment. What did she mean by that?

Everyone was frozen in place, as though waiting for something terrible to happen. They were all looking at him.

"If you will not tell them the truth, I will," said the Mother of Kish. "The day that your land died was the day that Pitirim the fool disappeared. None of you bothered to ask where he had gone, did you? You were content that he should be the scapegoat for your troubles."

She scanned the crowd, as though looking for something in the faces of the men. But they looked away from her like flowers closing their petals after sunset.

"What happened was this, as told me by a soldier who escaped with his life only because he was a coward. Three of my illustrious men at arms attacked old Pitirim in the woods. Evidently, they had had enough of his games. What they hadn't planned for was that their murder was witnessed by this young man."

She pointed at Andry. Her finger was slightly bent, as though it had been broken and grown back together crooked. It was a discordant note in the music of her beauty.

"He rushed to try to stop the fight, but what could a boy of ten do? He only got himself hurt in the tussle. Enough to draw blood, enough for that blood to fall to the earth..."

She accented that last part, as though it was the most important. Andry's heart beat wildly. He thought he understood what she was about to say. But no, it couldn't be. It just couldn't be.

"As soon as the blood fell to earth, that boy turned into a monster. He unleashed his secret power and destroyed my three warriors, plunging them alive into tombs of earth."

Whatever Andry had expected, it certainly wasn't *that*. He almost laughed at the absurdity of it.

The black-skinned warriors unsheathed their swords, all at the same time. Like loping wolves, they ran into the crowd as the men pushed and shoved each other to try to avoid them. All fifteen of the warriors surrounded Yan and Andry. Two of them took Yan roughly and dragged him to the feet of the Mother of Kish. Her eyes blazed like stars in a moonless sky as she looked at Yan prostrate before her.

"Will you not tell them *what* he is?" She waited for effect, though clearly Papa was not about to answer her. Not with the booted foot of one of the warriors on his neck. "Very well. I will show them. This is what happens to those who harbor monsters in the midst of paradise."

She turned to Budzislav and nodded. Budzislav picked up a metal collar that looked as heavy as a yoke. It unhinged at a point, opening up like a claw. As the warriors held Yan down, Budzislav put the collar on Papa. It clicked into place with a finality like death. He yanked Papa's head up, with the collar secured. Then he whispered something, as though speaking to the collar. It shimmered with red light, then began to glow.

Papa screamed in agony.

Andry's body rushed toward his father, but two warriors held him in place. Yan screamed again. His face was ashen, its skin loose, as though it were being pulled off his face.

Andry tried to fight off the warriors, but they didn't even move. He looked at Apsat. The old man wasn't looking at him, avoiding his gaze. But the kestrel looked straight at him.

Andry concentrated all his thoughts at the bird of prey.

WHY?

She cocked her head, opened her beak. Her tongue darted out as her wings unfurled and her shoulder feathers bunched up. She looked about to launch off Apsat's hand.

But then Apsat looked at her and shook his head, once. She

settled back into his arm, looking back at Andry for a moment with her too-human green eyes. Then she turned away.

Andry was alone.

But no, he wasn't alone.

Dunai, please. I can't stand this any more.

The earth shuddered under their feet.

The Mother of Kish's eyes lit up with joy and recognition. Then, her expression turned feral, like a mother bear facing down an attacking male trying to hurt her cub.

And Andry understood.

It was a trap.

Dunai, no!

But it was too late. The wind whipped the hair across their faces, birds screamed all around them, and the roaring began. Dunai was coming to protect her own.

Three white wolves the size of bears burst into the square, their slavering maws already bloody. Andry looked back to see the perfect line of spearmen buckling, with some of them grabbing their arms and legs with bloody hands.

"Apsat, *now!*" commanded the Mother of Kish.

Apsat's face was set. He looked utterly terrifying. Then, for a brief moment, he looked at Andry. And there was nothing but love in those eyes. And a request, as clear as though he had spoken into Andry's mind.

Trust me.

Andry reeled. Nothing made sense any more.

Apsat opened his arms wide, as though he would embrace the entire world in them. He closed his eyes and began to sing. The wolves fell asleep, the wind died down, and the birds stopped singing. But the tension was still like a string about to burst, humming higher and higher.

"Do you see whom you have been harboring, people of Dunai?" said the Mother of Kish, her eyes again sad and consoling, motherly as before. "That boy. He is a dark sorcerer the likes of which has not appeared on this earth since the days of Voran the Warrior."

Andry couldn't believe his ears. He almost laughed aloud at the stupidity of her words. But then, he saw the faces of his fellow villagers. They were cold, full of fear. Fear of *him*.

"So you see, now. Enemies at your borders, and an even darker enemy within. I can protect you from both." She pointed at the wolves for emphasis. "But you must accept me as your mother. You will all be my children. And I... *protect*... my children."

A commotion on the edge of the square distracted everyone. Elania, dressed like a woman, not a girl, her hair askew and her face strangely reddened with paint along the edge of her cheek, ran through the crowd, completely oblivious to the bloody soldiers, the sleeping wolves, the horse-the-size-of-a-house, or Yan and Andry being held captive.

"They're here!" she screamed. "They're in the village already!"

Andry smelled burning thatch. He tried to turn around, but the warriors still held him fast.

"Decide!" screamed the Mother of Kish. For the first time, she looked not in control of the situation. It seemed the news was unexpected to her as well. "Will you be my children?"

Every one of the heads of the Dunai families agreed.

Then, chaos.

Andry felt it like an explosion inside himself. In a single moment, all the animals of Dunai, all the insects, all the plants and trees—everything that had been blocked off from him for weeks—burst back into his mind with their smells, their calls, and most of all, their fury.

With a tingling sensation that was at the same time sinking terror and exhilaration, Andry knew why he had not sensed Dunai for so long.

She had been storing all her power for this moment.

The wolves all woke up at the same time and roared. Along the edges of the square, shimmering clouds of wasps gathered like thunderheads. Creeping vines with thorns the size of a man's index finger burst through the cracks between the cobblestones, reaching for Dunaian and invader alike. Vultures circled overhead, spinning faster and faster, making Andry dizzy.

"Apsat!" screamed the Mother of Kish. "Contain her!"

But Apsat was nowhere to be seen.

Andry realized that the warriors who had been holding him were cocooned in vines that constricted them like huge snakes. He ran toward his father, but his father was gone as well.

Turning quickly, he ran out of the square through a pandemonium of people rushing around without apparently any knowledge of where they were going.

He had reached the edge of the village when he saw the first wolf rider.

The wolf was sleek grey, with powerful muscles showing even through the rippling fur. Its eyes were red-rimmed, almost rabid-looking. On top of it, in a strange saddle with loops for the feet, was something that looked human... mostly. It had no hair, its skin was grey like stone, and it had eyes like abysses. It wore no armor, but both hands clutched curved swords that dripped with blood. It flew past Andry as though it didn't see him, into a knot of Karilan soldiers who tried to fight it off with spears.

Andry didn't wait to see the end of the attack. All around him, the fighting was intense. Buildings burned everywhere, the smoke making things seem even more nightmare-like than they already were. He ran and ran, trying to find a clear path to his house. When he reached the wheat fields, he saw his house.

Or rather, what remained of it. Two walls, burning fiercely, still stood. Everything else was black char and ash on the ground.

Andry fell on his knees in front of the ruin of his house. He wanted to die.

Not yet. Come to me.

He closed his eyes, and she stood before him as she had before, extending the bouquet of acanthia blossoms to him.

All is not lost. Come home.

He knew what she meant. She meant the place of his birth.

Andry's body felt like lead. But he forced himself to get up and move.

When he arrived at the stand of birches and alders, he saw the fairy ring of acanthia blossoms, glowing pink in the sun. There was no smoke anywhere to be seen, no sound of battle, no smell of burning wood and flesh.

He approached the circle with trepidation. He felt like being in church at a midnight service after being awoken unexpectedly, his body groggy but his mind on fire. In the middle of the fairy ring was a hole of utter blackness. Or so it seemed at first. As he came closer, he saw that it was a large burrow, big enough for an adult to fit through. It smelled of mushroom stew and wet leaves and cut grass.

Come. It is safe here.

He entered the fairy circle and crouched to all fours as he fit into the burrow. It felt like he was being swallowed. In utter terror, he stopped, unable to move for a full minute. But then, he thought he saw a glimmer of light in the distance of the burrow. In that glimmer, he saw the walls of the burrow widening ahead of him enough for him to stand. That made it easier, though he had to touch the sides of the passageway to convince himself he wasn't dreaming. The dripping stickiness of earthwormy soil cooled his fingertips. As he touched it, he thought he heard a sound like a whisper or like wind rustling through yellowing alder leaves in the autumn.

He walked forward. The glimmering half-light resolved into torchlight in the hand of someone standing in a chamber made of stones piled up on top of each other so perfectly that it seemed built by hand instead of a natural cave. The person holding the torch was Apsat. His kestrel sat on his shoulder and *kreeked* loudly when Andry walked into the cavern.

As he did, Mama shrieked and Papa groaned as they ran to him, enfolding him inside their embrace so that he felt he was in her womb again. He didn't notice he was crying until his nose tickled from the snot.

They were safe. Thank the Heights. They were safe.

"Papa?" he asked, reaching for his neck tentatively.

Papa pulled on the fringe of his collar and showed him. Even in the dancing firelight, Andry saw there was not a sign of the torture on his neck.

"It was a trick of the mind," said Yan, shuddering from the memory. "Some dark magic that makes you feel the pain, but leaves no traces on the skin."

"I'm so sorry, Andry," said Mama. "I should never have let this happen. It's all my fault."

Andry laughed. It was typical of Mama to take the weight of the world on her shoulders.

But Mama stayed deadly serious. She took him by the hand and walked him away from Papa and Apsat to a large stone jutting from the wall where they could sit together.

"There's something you need to know," she said, looking him directly in the eyes. "Something I meant to tell you when you were older."

Andry's heart stopped for a moment as all the words of the Mother of Kish flooded back into his mind. Dark sorcerer. Monster.

And in that moment, he considered for the first time that maybe she had been telling the truth. Maybe he was a monster. Maybe this was all *his* fault.

Mama seemed to intuit some of his thoughts, because she immediately hugged him and shushed him like a child.

"No, my darling. It's not your fault. Listen. I have to tell you a story.

"You were not simply born under an open sky on a purple morning. You died under an open sky on a purple morning."

CHAPTER

EIGHT

A FRUITFUL DARKNESS

Andry sat in place, letting the coolness of the stones seep into his back muscles. He ached all over, a pain he noticed only when he breathed out, as his mother finished telling him the truth of his birth.

How for years she had hidden the truth even from herself, preferring not to remember. How finally the dreams forced her to recall that he had not simply been born inside the ring of acanthia flowers. That he had been born in a rush of blood, some of it his own. His umbilical cord had torn, and he had had a loop of it around his neck. He would not breathe, no matter what she did.

Finally, she had put him on the earth in utter despair. It felt like her life had ended.

But then, the earth awoke.

That was the only way she could describe it. The blood had all gone, seeped into the earth as though the soil had drunk it like water. The umbilical cord had fallen off him. Then, he breathed, his grey skin filling with pink color like wine filling an empty wineskin. He screamed louder than any baby she had ever heard.

It was shortly after that, when he had found her breast and

she had found her joy again, that his father and sisters had found them.

"Dunai gave you her life," finished Mother.

"That is not the whole truth," said Apsat, coming up behind them.

Andry knew it. "We gave *her* life first, and she shared it back with us."

Apsat smiled sadly and nodded once.

"So it wasn't the Living Water from Vasyllia after all?" Andry looked up at Apsat, feeling more than a little faint, his hands shaking visibly in his lap.

"It *was* the Living Water that gave Dunai her fruitfulness. Her ability to bind together all the creatures that lived within her land, her *womb*, you might say. But what happened at your birth is something more. She came awake. She became... she became a person."

"I don't understand. Like a human?" asked Andry.

"To be a person, you need not necessarily be a human," said Apsat. "And not every human being is a person." Andry didn't understand. He would have to think about that. Later.

"That still doesn't explain..." said Mama, but she didn't finish, her eyes wide and full of fear again as she saw something behind them.

"It doesn't explain," said Budzislav from the far side of the cavern. "What exactly Dunai wants with your little boy. And what she is willing to do to get it."

Several things happened at once. Budzislav reached both hands out, and stones started to fall out of the walls, showering earth on their heads. Mama cried out and tried to cover Andry with her body. The kestrel flew off Apsat's shoulder and attacked Budzislav, her talons reaching for his eyes. Apsat's face turned white as milk, his mouth opening as though he would scream, but nothing came out. Budzislav's smile turned bestial, and he flicked a finger at the kestrel. A stone flew from the floor of the cavern and struck the bird in mid-air.

It fell to the earth crookedly, one wing broken under its body.

Apsat cried out in fury and began to run toward Budzislav, but froze in place as Budzislav shook his index finger at Apsat. Another stone flew from the wall and stopped an inch away from the head of the kestrel, hovering in mid-air, shuddering as though teetering at the edge of an abyss.

"We have an agreement," said Budzislav. "*I* have not broken it, and I am willing to believe that you acted out of haste, without thinking. I will not kill her. But you must carry out your end of the bargain."

The stones in the cavern groaned, as though they were alive. The earth shuddered, and dirty rain fell on them again. The strain in the air was palpable. Any minute now, the cavern would collapse.

"Don't wait too long, Apsat," said Budzislav. Blood dripped from his nose. His body was strained, taut, like a stick about to snap in half.

Then, the air seemed to shimmer like the surface of a lake. The kestrel's form lost its firmness, evaporating like mist. But instead of disappearing, it transformed into a human girl, her hair filthy and tangled, her arm stuck under her body in a painful way. She moaned, softly. Then she moved her head, just enough for Andry to see her face. Although it was pale, racked with pain, and filthy, the resemblance was uncanny.

"She's your daughter," said Andry. He knew now why Apsat did the Mother's bidding.

Apsat's head snapped toward him. "You can see her?" His eyes were wide with surprise.

"Of course! Can't everyone?" Andry looked around. But everyone's eyes were confused. No one saw the girl, it seemed, only the kestrel.

Then Andry felt it. The presence, not diffuse like it usually was. Dunai was here. In the strongest, most complete fullness of what she was. She filled his mind with her thoughts, filled his body with her own self, filled his breath with the wind of the trees, filled his eyes with the light of the sun on a winter morning. He felt simultaneously tiny and huge, in two places at once. His head exploded in pain like a poker shoved into his temple.

He closed his eyes and saw Dunai before him, her dress like flower petals bent by the wind. Her eyes were full of a single question. A request. A need.

"What do you want from me, Dunai?"

She opened her mouth and...

...the world exploded in a shower of dirt, water, and air.

Andry was pushed to the ground by a gale, but he resisted and willed himself to look up.

The cavern roof was gone, and he saw clouds swirling in the sky directly above him. The lip of the cavern wall was ringed with huge teeth—no, it was soldiers with spears. None of them looked down into the hole, but *up*. Up, at something floating down from the sky, its wings unfurled and flapping strangely in the wind. No, not wings. The edges of a billowing, saffron-colored robe. The Mother of Kish had found them.

Andry looked back at his family. They were pressed against one of the remaining stone walls of the former cavern, though he couldn't tell if they were being held there by some power or just cowering in fear. Apsat crouched over his daughter, the stone that had hung over her head no longer there. Budzislav was on his knees, his eyes lowered. Andry saw a glimpse of those eyes as he lowered them. They were no longer dead amber. They were shot through with devotion, softened with adoration. He worshiped the Mother as she descended on the air.

For a moment, Andry remembered Mama's stories of the vila, their carnivorous maws filled with razor-teeth even as they sang beautiful songs of love and loss. The Mother of Kish reminded him of those stories.

She landed in front of Andry, having eyes for no one but him. Her eyes were wide and beautiful and utterly mad.

"Andry, my child. Would you like to meet your mother? Your *true* mother?"

Andry didn't move, didn't speak, didn't so much as breathe.

The Mother of Kish turned to Apsat, who was weeping over his daughter, kissing her unbroken hand. Her eyes were closed, but she moaned in pain, her face twitching every few minutes.

"It is not too late for her, Apsat," said the Mother of Kish. "You can still save her."

Apsat looked at Andry with eyes that implored him for … something. Andry didn't know what. He wanted to give it to him with all his heart. But what could he do? He was only a boy.

Apsat looked away from Andry, back to his daughter's face, then he shook his head. The weeping racked him with sobs.

Do something.

It was Dunai, speaking to him. He closed his eyes and saw her.

"You are the one with the power," Andry answered.

Don't you understand? I am nothing without you.

"I'm so tired, Dunai. It's not fair. I'm only a boy."

I have made a paradise for you. Not for your people, for you. For you, Andry.

"Why?"

Don't you understand?

He felt her retreat from him into herself. She was weeping. Apsat was weeping. Mama was weeping. And all because of him.

It wasn't fair.

"Make it stop," he said, aloud.

"I will," said the Mother of Kish. He looked up at her face. She was weeping, too, the tears of a true mother. She would fix everything. Everything would be well again.

"But you need to help me," said the Mother of Kish.

"Tell me what to do," he said, feeling the earth firming underneath him. Just a little longer, and everything would be well again.

"It will hurt, but you are strong. I believe in you. Here, take my hands."

She extended them. They were soft-looking, somewhat pudgy, inviting.

He took them. They were warm.

"Apsat, this is the time. Now, or you lose her forever."

Apsat's head drooped to his chest. With an almost flaccid gesture, he twisted his hands in a way similar to what he did when the goldfinch came back to life.

Dunai cried out in his mind. It sounded like pain.

The floor of the cavern was now covered in acanthia flowers, growing like weeds. The flowers were breathing—in and out, in and out—their breath visible as golden, pollen-like spores. The spores filled the space of the cavern, and Andry was afraid he would choke on them. But, as before, the golden dust was too small to be felt on the tongue or in the nose. It danced on the air in whorling patterns.

"Look," said the Mother of Kish.

Andry was no longer in that place. As before, he was in another place entirely. He saw Elania again. She was sitting outside her father's smithy on her knees in mud. Her hands were covered with the mud, her face streaked with it. She wept and cried out, but he heard nothing. There was nothing remaining of the smithy except an outline of smoldering rocks. Andry thought he could see the form of a body inside the tumble of stones and bits of metal and charred wood, but he wasn't sure of it.

His heart felt like it was going to tear itself apart.

"This is what will happen, Andry, to the whole world. I understand the Nebesti, I do. For so many years, they were prevented from being who they were. Their language was put down; their songs were suppressed. Their stories were polluted with official, Karilan-safe versions. Their history was forgotten. Of course they lashed out."

Andry wanted to close his eyes, to shut out the vision of Elania's pain. But what waited for him behind his closed eyes—Dunai's inexplicable request—was even worse. He could look nowhere, turn nowhere.

"But they went too far. They allied with powers that have no love for human beings. Powers that would chew the world and spit it out. Then dance on its corpse for sheer brazenness."

"Why are you showing me this?"

"Because only you can stop this."

He was back in the cavern, amid the acanthia flowers that grew in even greater profusion than before.

"It was your blood that connected you to Dunai when you were born. That connection is the strongest force in this Realm of Earth, Andry. What the two of you can do together is remarkable. I can use it to save Elania. To save hundreds of Elanias in hundreds of villages like this that will fall before the fury of this new army. Will you let me protect your people? Will you let me protect Dunai? I only need a bit of your blood."

Yes. She was a mother to all. It was right for her to do it. Andry couldn't do it. He had no magic.

He was no monster.

That thought was like awakening from a dream by falling.

The Mother of Kish had caused all the problems to begin with. She had called him a monster publicly, had accused him of killing three soldiers. She had had Papa tortured before his own son! And now, she wanted him to believe that *she* would protect Dunai? That she was the healer of a wound she had inflicted herself? If she had never turned her motherly gaze on Dunai, this war would never have come here.

Things would have remained as they always were.

But that wasn't right, either. No, things were not good in Dunai, so much was clear. The occupation had only revealed what was already true. The rot at the heart of Dunai. He would never want to go back to the way things were, not now that he knew the hearts of his fellow Dunaians.

For the first time in his life, Andry felt he had no home. He had nowhere to go. He didn't know what to do.

There was one thing he could do. One thing left. He could do what his fellow Dunaians refused to do.

He could defy the Mother of Kish.

He realized he was still holding her hands. With revulsion, he tossed them aside.

"You are no mother. You are a snake. I will never do what you want. I know you will do terrible things to me. I know you can cause pain. But you will never have this blood of mine. Not while I live."

The Mother of Kish now had a face of stone. Her eyebrows seemed etched in place like thin, arrogant scratches in granite.

"I gave you a chance to give me your blood willingly. You chose not to take it."

"Yes, *I* choose."

He closed his eyes. Dunai stood there in his mind's eye, her eyes wide, her hands extended, her face set. She was ready to overturn the earth itself to protect him. In his mind's eye, he shook his head.

No, Dunai. Don't play her game. Let me go.

A sharp pain in his left arm. He opened his eyes. A red streak crossed his left forearm. It dripped blood onto the ground. The Mother of Kish held his arm in a grip like a vise. Her other hand held a white bone knife that was now edged in his blood. Her eyes were no longer human. They seemed to glow with fury.

"I will do *anything* to protect my children," she whispered.

As the blood dripped, Andry could feel Dunai retreating from him, leaving him behind. The ever-present hum of wild animal and plant life that had been the background noise of his life faded. The lives of other creatures, their strange desires and joys —he reached out to them, but they curled away from him like fern fronds closing in on themselves. He was Andry, son of Yan. And nothing more.

It was far more painful than the cut on his arm.

"Thank you, my boy," said a voice behind him, familiar somehow, but also different. Like something heard in a dream a long time ago. "Thank you for your sacrifice."

A golden light filled the roofless cavern, blotting out the sun entirely. The Mother of Kish cried out in pain and let Andry's arm go. She tried to cover her eyes, but the light seemed to burn her as well as blind her.

Andry turned around, surprised that he could see in that light. All around him, everyone was flat on their faces, their forms mostly concealed by the acanthia blossoms that had grown to the height of his hip. The light was coming from where Apsat had stood before. Instead of Apsat, a warrior armed in ancient chain mail stood. There was a spinning sun of red gold on his chest, and his hair was long and white. His eyes were stars, and he wore no helmet. From his extended right hand, a small sapling grew, its roots wrapped around his wrist. Its branches were aflame, but it did not burn. Two wings of shimmering red gold extended out from his back. Andry understood now what the Karilan mounted warriors with their swan-wing banners were trying to imitate.

Next to this transfigured version of Apsat stood a girl about Andry's own age with dark hair, fiery brown eyes, and a smile that was a challenge to the world.

But that image faded along with the light, and once again Apsat was as he was before, though the smile of his daughter was still a challenge to the world.

"Budzislav!" cried the Mother of Kish, now on her knees before Apsat. "The bargain! Kill them both!"

Budzislav could do nothing more than gurgle an indistinct answer. He was asleep in a bed made of Dunai's spores. He had a contented, stupid smile on his face.

"You are bound by blood, Apsat!" She hissed the "s" of his name unnaturally. "By the ancient magic of the Deathless. You cannot break free! This is not possible!"

"There is an older magic still, Mother. Have you forgotten what land you stand on? This is Vasyllia of old. In Vasyllia, the law of sacrifice is king."

Andry laughed aloud. He knew who Apsat was, now.

"You are Voran the Warrior!" he could hardly contain his excitement.

"I am Voran the Healer," answered Apsat, and pointed at Andry's arm. There was a scar on his forearm, but no wound.

The Mother of Kish stood up, though it seemed her body was

almost too heavy to move. Through a force of will that was stamped by a fierce expression of hatred, she raised her hands. The fringes of her cloak billowed around her as though she were the center of a whirlwind.

"You should not have revealed yourself, old man," she croaked. Then she grabbed the arm of Budzislav and sliced open his forearm.

He screamed as he came awake. Almost before their eyes, his skin lost its color and its thickness, becoming shriveled and old before their eyes, as though he were aging in minutes, not decades. His mustache drooped and his hair went white. His voice was no more than a croak. He fell awkwardly to his side, dead.

The Mother of Kish was renewed, her eyes bright again and able to pierce Voran's light. She faced him, no longer afraid or in pain.

"You may have won this round, old man. But know this. I will not rest until I have taken this boy's power. No one else will have it, certainly not you. And there's another thing you probably should know. Your old friend sends his greetings. The Deathless One is coming."

She raised her hands as though she were reaching up to catch a rope dangling from the edge of the cavern's lip. Impelled upward as though by a rope Andry couldn't see, she flew into the sky. The spears around the lip of the hole retreated.

"What did she mean?" asked Andry.

Andry saw that the old warrior's brow was furrowed in thought.

"It can't be, can it?" he said, to no one in particular.

His daughter answered. She had a voice like a bell. Andry liked it at once. "If you could leave Vasyllia-of-the-Mountains to come here, then perhaps the Raven can escape his bonds?"

"It's possible, I suppose. A long time has passed."

"But what about Dunai?" asked Andry. "Can't we do something to save Dunai?"

Voran snapped awake and smiled. "Oh, Andry. You're a marvel. Yes, yes, of course we can."

※

VORAN and his daughter held a short and secretive conference with Andry's parents, in which there was much furtive glancing from Mama at Andry. But Andry was having a hard time keeping his attention on them, though his mind warned him that he might have to pay for it later. Especially with Mama. But now that the Mother of Kish had gone, along with her foul magic, Dunai's pain inundated him like loud, insistent music that forced all thoughts away from the mind. He wanted to do nothing but lie face-down, with his arms outstretched on the ground, every inch of him covering as much of Dunai's soil-body as he could.

But he had asked her to let him go. Her music was like the scar in a wound created by their parting.

All around him, the acanthia flowers still bloomed, though they shuddered in no wind, and some seemed to wilt at the red edges. Where the stones of the broken cavern interrupted the perfect line of flowers, they looked like cliffs standing in the midst of churning waves.

That detail gave him an idea, even as he dropped to his knees, too tired to keep himself standing any more.

"Voran," he said. His voice sounded like the voice of an old man. "This place. It is special to Dunai. Heal her, please."

Voran appeared at his side. There were no whispers behind him, where Mama and Papa had stood. Hopefully they were well.

"I will, Andry," said Voran in a half-whisper. "That is the least of what I can do for you and your fiery heart."

Andry closed his eyes. He wanted to sleep more than anything. Dunai didn't appear to him. Instead, he heard that same music as before, when Voran had brought the goldfinch back to life. The music was huge and joyfully sad. Andry sensed the cavern close up again. It was like a huge old grandmother knitting the pieces of the world back together.

Andry sighed. Some of his tiredness sloughed off him with that sigh.

When he was ready to open his eyes, he saw that the walls of the cavern—completely whole again—were covered in reddish dots of light that gleamed, fading to a dark half-light, then intermittently flaring to something like the light of a large bonfire. The air smelled like roasted potatoes and squash with a dash of thyme. Only at the edge of that smell could he still sense an afterglow of sickly sweet rot, like overripe tomatoes. Voran sat across from him in the sea of acanthia that glowed pink in the changing light. It was warm, but not the sticky wet-summer kind of warm. More like a homely, late autumn hearth-fire kind of warm that caressed the skin.

Voran smiled. Andry realized he had not really seen Voran smile until that moment. Apsat's smile was different—careful and hopeful, but always worried. Voran's eyes almost glowed, his smile was so ardent.

"Andry, you have a great gift. How you can't see it astounds me. You have something like a second, inner sight. You see the highest world, the Realm of Aer, as it intertwines with the Realm of Earth. You see the way things are, not the way things seem. It is a very rare kind of magic. Even I, who can cross the worlds through places where there are no doors, even I have never encountered it before. So only you can reach out to Dunai, because only you can see her. She will tell you what she needs."

"But she has left me. I asked her to."

"She loves you, Andry. No mother ever abandons her own child."

Andry nodded. It felt right, what Voran said. He closed his eyes and tried to open his other sight. Dimly, he saw a wide plain covered in undulating grasses with pink and purple wildflowers interspersed among the different shades of green. Dunai was a bowshot away, her back turned to him. He walked toward her, but did not come any closer. It was as though he walked in place.

She would not make this easy for him.

"Voran, will you come with me?" asked Andry, his eyes still closed.

Voran stood next to him on the same plain. He was young, his hair and beard dark, almost black, giving his green eyes a haunted look, as though there were a fire deep within them.

"Yes," he said.

Andry breathed deeply, trying to still himself as Papa had taught him. He tried to put himself in Dunai's place, to see as she saw, as Mama had taught him. It was too much. The hugeness of it all.

"Dunai, will you come back to me?" he asked.

She shook her head.

"I will give you my life if I can. Willingly."

She turned to him, and her eyes were frightening in their pain and their need and their love.

Do not say it. You do not know what you say.

Voran let a small sigh escape. Andry saw that it wasn't sadness. Voran had realized something surprising.

"My lady," Voran said, "let me tell you a story. I once knew an old woodsman whose whole life was dedicated to the forests below Vasyllia-that-was. All he ever did was prune old branches and sing songs to the seedlings and clear out dry brush for the bluebells to grow. He once told me of a certain kind of gorse bush. The farmers hated it, because it grew like a weed. But they could never kill it completely. It kept coming back.

"One year, there was a fire in the forest after a lightning strike. The Vasylli are expert woodsmen, but they could only do so much. After the fire had had its way with the forest, there were gaps of scorched earth like scabs on the mountainside. But the next year, I was surprised to find everything covered in gorse. When the farmers came out with their picks and shovels to kill it, the old woodsman stopped them in anger.

" 'Don't you understand?' he said to them. 'The forest is coming back.'

"I didn't understand what he was talking about at first. The truth came out later a few years later. Under the cover of that weed, all the seedings of a new wood had grown, protected from the sun's heat. They grew so fast, it was astounding. The young trees soon covered the gorse in their own shadows."

Dunai didn't answer, but it seemed her shoulders grew even more tense.

"The gorse, deprived of the sun it needed to live, died soon afterward. And it never came back in that part of the forest. A new, young, strong forest grew in its place, filled with more living things than I had ever seen before or afterward."

Dunai turned to Voran. Her tears sparkled like starlight in a pool.

Yes. I am dying. I have been dying ever since Andry was born. And it is right that I should. Andry is indeed a young, strong forest. He will fill this land more than I ever did.

Andry found it hard to breathe.

But Andry gave me of his own life, and I came awake in a way I had not for thousands of generations... I don't want to die. I want to live.

Andry wanted to say something to comfort her, but he forced himself to wait. To be still. Finally, she looked at him. Her eyes were like pools that have no bottom to them. It terrified him.

Andry, my son. I thought that if you allowed me into your body, I could... inhabit it. Like a house. I could have a form. A body.

His heart chilled in his chest. If she had entered him like that, there wouldn't have been anything left of himself. She would have devoured him. She was too big to fit in his body.

But then he saw it all from her eyes, and her grief and regret flooded him.

"I love you, Mother," he whispered.

Voran spoke. "Dunai, you are the womb of this land. The mother that feeds people and animals and plants. You will never truly die, not while the land survives."

But I will no longer be... a person.

It was not a question.

"No. You will return to the way you were before Andry was born."

She did not answer, but her face was eloquent. It said, "It is not enough."

It was terrible. She either had to accept the death of her consciousness to continue the life of the land, or she had to invade a foreign body like a parasite.

But then, Andry had an idea. "But what if she could have both?"

Her expression was like a sunrise.

CHAPTER

NINE

THE OLDEST MAGIC OF ALL

In the land of Dunai, the end of the growing season is also marked by an unusual event. Many places can boast of sunsets that become more glorious the closer the winter comes. You may have even seen such a sunset yourself. But hardly anyone outside Dunai has seen its golden sunset.

The final sunset of Dunai's summer transfigures the air into a sea of molten gold, dusted with dappled gemstones. The clouds erupt in layers of colors that have no name in human language. It is as if the sky opens up like a door, and beyond it is another, far greater sky. As though the Realm of Aer, for a moment, is visible from the earth.

Yan and Pelaghia awaited the golden sunset with some trepidation. Nothing about this summer had gone according to pattern. There had been no harvest festival, only an invasion. The land had lost her rich fruitfulness. Hardly a building had been left standing by the battle between the forces of Karila and Nebesta, a battle that had left no clear winner, only corpses.

The land itself seemed to have been afflicted and wounded. Smoking fissures that smelled of rotten eggs gouged the fields of wheat. Huge monoliths, seemingly pushed up from under the earth, loomed in between the ruins of the granaries. Black scabs covered the hills where fires had eaten up all that lived.

No one was sure how they would survive the coming winter.

One evening, Yan and Pelaghia watched the distant tips of the trees on the hills as the sunlight faded. It was the hour of dusk when the edges of the trees were so sharp, they seemed to cut into the fading orange of the sky.

"Have you heard the latest one?" asked Yan, reaching for Pelaghia's hand. She obliged, and pressed herself against his bulk, her head on his shoulder.

"Let me guess. The end of the world has come, and soon the Realm of Earth will perish in fire."

He looked at her with mock astonishment. "How did you know?"

They both smiled, but the warmth they felt was only in the closeness of their bodies.

"How long do you think we have?" asked Pelaghia.

"Of peace? They'll leave us alone for a time. But they'll be back."

"Do you think he'll manage it?" asked Pelaghia, her eyes hungry for only one possible answer.

Yan's smiled deepened, and her eyes softened again.

"He was born on a purple morning. Of course he'll manage it."

THE NEXT MORNING, Yan got up early and began to till the late-summer earth. Pelaghia looked at him with that crooked smile she wore when she thought he was being ridiculous, but then she reached for her spade. They planted a late crop of beans, potatoes, and winter squashes.

It was good to work again.

Soon afterward, they took in Goran, who had survived and who had saved Elania from her captors. His wife, her mother, had perished in the flames. Kira befriended Elania immediately, and slowly, the young girl found something like her old smile again. Yan and Goran took the lead in organizing the remaining Dunaian men—many had been taken prisoner or killed—to gathering what they could of the trampled grain into the remaining granaries, to rebuilding what could be rebuilt before the winter, to helping the old and infirm settle in at least some comfort. By some miracle, the common house with its storyteller's firepit and its many rooms was still standing, with the walls only slightly browned from fire. The foundation was good, Yan confirmed, and even the thatch was only scorched.

Pelaghia and the girls took charge of what became a kind of infirmary in the common house. The bandages and salves helped, of course, but Pelaghia's calm, firm determination and Elania's new-found smile did more to heal the wounded. Voran's daughter, whose name was Predislava, told funny stories by the firepit that left even the most wounded grabbing their sides in mixed hilarity and pain. She was clearly enjoying being the center of attention.

Pelaghia could see that Andry liked her very much indeed.

But he was too busy with his mysterious errand to spend much time with the women. Every morning, he and Voran left to walk up into the hills. They would be gone most of the day, often returning after nightfall with bright eyes and filthy hands.

Every time Pelaghia asked Voran what they were doing, he smiled mischievously and bent his head at Andry, who only giggled.

It was strange to hear such a sound come from her old-souled little son. Her strange hero.

The golden sunset came, even more brilliant than in previous years. Or perhaps their suffering had left them more vulnerable to its beauty.

As soon as it began, Andry started singing an old song that Pelaghia used to sing to him. It left smiles on the faces of all whom he passed as he ran toward the infirmary. How different a reaction that was, compared to a time when they had watched him with the typical fear and mistrust of the strange that made some even hate him, because they didn't understand him.

But Andry hardly noticed. He had more important things to do.

You can probably easily imagine him, all ten years of unbridled enthusiasm, rushing hither and thither, getting all the able-bodied young men to help the wounded and the sick up out of their beds and onto their feet.

"It's time," he said.

As easy as Andry is to imagine, you may have a more difficult time imagining the procession of the halt and the sick and the old as they tottered and limped and half-crawled up difficult mountain trails behind a boy who bounded ahead of them like a faun enjoying its first spring. There he ran, Voran and Predislava directly behind him, both with their eyes glowing with some kind of secret knowledge. Yan and Pelaghia and Kira and Aglusha behind them, almost in awe of their strange little Andry. Behind them, the mass of wounded pushing forward, in spite of the pain and exhaustion.

The procession, like a stream of industrious ants, made its way to the lookout where the mountain range grew up into the clouds and beyond them, to the invisible city of Vasyllia above.

Andry turned to all the wounded. Their gazes were tired, confused. Some were hopeful.

"Just a little further!" he called to them.

They walked along the ridge to a clearing in the fir trees. There, on a spur of exposed rock, stood a strange kind of statue. There were vines there, and roots, and flowers, and tubers, and green things. There was mud, and humus, and soil, and bark, and flowers, and roots. It looked like it had not been made by hands, but grown from the earth itself.

As indeed it had. Here, finally revealed, was the long work of Andry and Voran. Every day, they had come to this place. Andry had seen her image in his mind. Voran had taught him the old songs of Vasyllia and how to use them to help natural things come together in new and unexpected ways. And, after weeks of exhausting work, it became a thing like a statue, taller than the tallest man, her face just as he saw it in his mind's eye, her dress a riot of blossoms. Her skin was brown like the earth, and it shimmered between the firmness of bark and the suppleness of vine. But her eyes were closed.

Voran touched Andry's shoulder.

"Are you ready, my boy?"

Andry smiled mischievously. "Are you?"

Voran shrugged and smiled. "We shall see."

Andry reached out his hand to Voran, and the other he left open, palm-up, extended toward the statue of Dunai he had sung into existence. He closed his eyes. There stood the living Dunai in his mind's eyes. She was covered in blossoms of orange and purple and light blue and white edged with red, as though she had put on a new dress. Her hair was not tangled, but woven like honeysuckle on a tree branch. Her smile was sheepish, the smile of a bride.

Voran began to sing. Andry joined him, letting the song go where it wanted as it poured out of him. Dunai breathed in deeply and sang. All around them, birdsong rose in a vast crescendo, along with the chittering of small beasts, the howling of wolves, the barking of foxes, and the neighing of horses. Never had such a vast choir sung such a harmony in Dunai.

Then, the earth shook underneath.

"Dunai," said Voran, "take our sorrows and our joys, our strength and our weakness. We give them to you willingly. For you are our mother. You are the true Deathless, who will not die while the earth lives."

Then all the wounded and all the sick cried out in pain. But it was short-lived, for their cries turned into expressions of shock and wonder. They looked at their wounds and their broken bones and their diseased members. They were all healed.

They all looked up at the form of Dunai, as made by Voran and Andry, and they gave thanks.

In Andry's mind, Dunai's face was drawn, even as she smiled, with eyes for no one but him. She looked ready to fall over at a breath of wind. That final healing had taken all her remaining strength.

"Voran, it's now or never," said Andry.

Voran shook his head once in slight doubt, then closed his eyes in concentration as his song deepened.

"Dunai," said Andry. "Come home."

For a long moment, everything went still. Everything went silent. The sun dipped behind the wall of the mountains. The golden sunrise ended.

Andry gasped. He felt Dunai's firm grip, horny and tough like the bark of a maple tree, in his outstretched hand. His eyes still closed, he listened intently. The great song of the animals of the Dunai hadn't stopped. She was still present in the land.

Shaking with excitement, he opened his eyes and looked up at the face he had sung into existence with Voran.

Dunai opened her eyes and smiled at him.

Sign up to my Readers' Inner Circle, and I'll send you:

1. My free first in series, *The Song of the Sirin,* which begins the story of Vasyllia and Voran, its greatest (and most flawed) hero, one thousand years before the events of *The Son of the Deathless.*

2. My story "Erestuna," a comic fantasy about the epic standoff between a seminarian, a bunch of Cossacks, and a seductive, very hungry mermaid.

3. A digital prize pack of art from the *Raven Son* series, including desktop wallpaper and a fantasy map in high definition.

You can get these gifts for free by signing up to my Readers' Inner Circle at https://nicholaskotar.com

ALSO BY NICHOLAS KOTAR

If you enjoyed *The Son of the Deathless,* you will definitely enjoy the earlier adventures of Voran in Vasyllia in the *Raven Son* series, available in ebook, paperback, and audiobook editions.

ABOUT THE AUTHOR

Nicholas Kotar is a writer of epic fantasy inspired by Slavic fairy tales, a freelance translator from Russian to English, the resident conductor of the men's choir at an Orthodox monastery in the middle of nowhere, and a semi-professional vocalist. His one great regret in life is that he was not born in the nineteenth century in St. Petersburg, but he is doing everything he can to remedy that error.